MY BIG FAT FATAL WEDDING

A SUNNY MEADOWS & KALLI BALLAS CROSSOVER

KARI LEE TOWNSEND

OLIVERHEBERBOOKS

All rights reserved.

No part of this publication may be sold, copied, distributed, reproduced or transmitted in any form or by any means, mechanical or digital, including photocopying and recording or by any information storage and retrieval system without the prior written permission of both the publisher, Oliver Heber Books and the author, Kari Lee Townsend, except in the case of brief quotations embodied in critical articles and reviews.

NO AI TRAINING: Without in any way limiting the author's [and publisher's] exclusive rights under copyright, any use of this publication to "train" generative artificial intelligence (AI) technologies and/or large language models to generate text, or any other medium, is expressly prohibited. The author reserves all rights to license uses of this work for the training and development of any generative AI and/or large language models.

PUBLISHER'S NOTE: This is a work of fiction. Names, characters, places, and incidents either are the product of the author's imagination or are used fictitiously. Any resemblance to actual persons, living or dead, business establishments, events, or locales is entirely coincidental.

My Big Fat Fatal Wedding Copyright 2025 © Kari Lee Townsend

Cover art by Dar Albert at Wicked Smart Designs

Published by Oliver-Heber Books

0 9 8 7 6 5 4 3 2 1

To my big, loud, loving family—thank you for the stories, the food, the drama, and the joy! We might not be Greek, but we sure know how to party like them. Opa! Forget ouzo ... cheers to the wine that got me through the rewrites 😉

1

KALLI

The tape measure dangled from my fingers like the thread of the Moirai, waiting to decide the garment's fate, as I squinted at the lace edging on my newest *Kalli Original*. Two millimeters. The trim was exactly two millimeters off-center, a microscopic flaw that might as well be a flashing neon sign to my perfectionist eye.

I adjusted it carefully, my breath held hostage in my lungs as I worked, making me worry about how that was affecting my insides. The quiet of my loft in my best friend's boutique was a temporary sanctuary that I knew—with the certainty of someone who was about to have her life hijacked by well-meaning loved ones—wouldn't last much longer.

Full Disclosure was empty of customers this morning, giving me precious time to arrange the front display rack with my latest designs before Jaz arrived for work. The morning light streaming through the windows caught on delicate silk and intricate lace, illuminating the careful craftsmanship I'd poured into each piece. I stepped back, tilting my head to assess the overall effect.

Perfect, except for that darn trim.

"This is what happens when you try to rush production," I muttered to myself, pinching the offensive edge between my fingertips. "Two millimeters might as well be two miles." I sighed. It would drive me crazy until I fixed it.

The bell above the front door jingled with such enthusiasm it might as well have been announcing the Second Coming, which, in a way, it was. Jazlyn Alvarez —my maid of honor extraordinaire—barreled through the entrance like a particularly fabulous hurricane.

We'd been best friends since we were kids but couldn't be more opposite.

"Kalliope Ballas, future Mrs. Nikos Stevens, prepare to have your mind blown!" Jaz announced, her arms overflowing with what appeared to be the entire contents of a wedding supply store.

Between her fingers, precariously balanced like circus performers on a tightrope, was one oat milk latte and one herbal tea. Her phone was wedged in what she called her bra pocket, and her oversized tote bag threatened to spill its contents with each bouncing step.

The most alarming item in her arsenal was a binder so thick it could stop a bullet. Its cover was decorated with glitter and emblazoned with "Kalli & Nik's Epic Wedding Extravaganza" in what appeared to be hand-painted gold lettering.

"I brought reinforcements," Jaz declared with a wink, depositing the beverages on the counter with surprising delicacy for someone whose entire being seemed to vibrate with excess energy.

Before I could respond, two more figures appeared in the doorway, and I felt my meticulous morning plans crumbling faster than phyllo dough in clumsy hands. I bit back a groan and pasted on a smile.

"Kalliope! We here!" Ma's voice filled the boutique, her arms laden with small mesh bags of what I immediately recognized as koufeta—the traditional sugar-coated almonds given as wedding favors. Her polyester pants swished with every step, swaying her massive beehive of teased black hair.

Behind her, Aunt Tasoula struggled with what looked like a rolled-up poster of considerable size. As usual, she wore her clothes two sizes too tight and ridiculously long hair extensions.

"We thought we find you here." Aunt Tasoula maneuvered the giant tube through the door with the determination of someone smuggling a body. "We bring concept art for you reception centerpieces. Okay? Okay."

I stared at the tube with trepidation. "Concept art?"

"Just a little something." Ma waved her hand dismissively. I noticed her fingers were dusted with powdered sugar, leaving faint trails in the air like ghostly contrails. "Yiayia and I stay up all night. We *so* excited. We have big surprise."

"Thanks, Ma." I gave her a hug, hearing her thoughts. *Aphrodite cradle a heart—symbolize you love! It so special like you.*

After a freak accident of falling out of my loft, I'd hit my head and suddenly was able to read people's minds but only when touching them.

A nightmare for a germaphobe like me.

"A seven-foot Aphrodite," Aunt Tasoula blurted, thumping the tube against the floor for emphasis. "Life-size. One for each table." She beamed proudly.

Ma glared at her sister for ruining the surprise.

My mouth opened, but no words emerged as I let go of Ma and took a step back, rubbing hand sanitizer into my palms.

Jaz, meanwhile, started to spread her collection of mood boards across the counter I'd so meticulously organized. Each one was a collage of images so densely packed they resembled artistic manifestations of anxiety—colors, fabrics, flowers, and venue options competing for attention in a visual shouting match.

I took several deep breaths.

"I've organized everything by theme," Jaz explained, pointing to each board in succession. "Mediterranean Sunset, Greek Goddess Glam, Modern Mythology, and—my personal favorite—Olympian Romance." She was so excited, I didn't have the heart to tell her they were stressing me out.

"They're … colorful," I managed, taking a cautious sip of the herbal tea she brought me, wincing at the heat. I appreciated her effort, but those boards weren't my thing. I shuddered, looking away, and set my tea down.

Ma bustled over to inspect the lingerie display, her sugar-dusted fingers hovering dangerously close to a cream-colored silk chemise that had taken me three weeks to perfect.

I lunged forward with the reflexes of a mother protecting her child. "Careful! The fabric—"

Too late. A light dusting of sugar transferred from her fingertips to the delicate silk, and I felt a corresponding twitch develop beneath my left eye.

"Oh, sorry, Kalliope," she said, not sounding particularly sorry at all. "Look at these koufeta! I find supplier. He make in seventeen colors. We coordinate with you bridesmaids' dresses. It nice. You see."

The bell jingled again, but this time it was just the

delivery guy with a box that Jaz signed for with a flourish.

"Perfect timing!" she squealed, snatching the box. "These are the sample wedding thank you cards. I ordered them in twelve different styles because I couldn't decide which font best captured your essence."

My phone vibrated in my pocket with a familiar ringtone—Chloe, Nik's ma, whose ability to create drama rivaled that of any Shakespearean actor.

"Kalli! I need picture of Yiayia's ring," she demanded before I could even say hello. "Jaz no answer her phone. I need to capture the vintage filigree to finish the custom ring box. You see?"

Jaz still had the antique piece that had been in Nik's family for generations because Chloe didn't trust Nik to watch it after losing it to mobsters during his bachelor party in Atlantic City. I'd heard all about the drama after Boomer spilled the beans to Jaz. Meanwhile, Chloe didn't trust herself not to lose the ring, either, so Jaz had been appointed the guardian. Nik had gotten the ring back from the mob, but at a price, since they had a grudge against Nik's partner, Boomer, who also happened to be Jaz's husband. But Boomer promised us both that the mob was no longer anything to worry about, which was good, because I didn't think I could handle any more worries.

I rubbed my aching temples. "Jaz sent you three pictures of the ring yesterday, Chloe."

"From different angles! I need one with natural light. And side profile." Chloe's exasperation flowed through the phone like a tangible force. "And make sure my Nikos no come near it. He bad boy."

"Well, he found it eventually, so everything is good

now." I closed my eyes and prayed to the gods for patience.

"Send picture soon. Love you!" She hung up before I could respond.

I turned back to the boutique chaos happening around me to find that it had multiplied exponentially in the thirty seconds I was distracted. The reason? Jaz's pets and mine had broken through the baby gate in the back room. We'd installed a doggie door that led to a small fenced-in yard behind the boutique for the times we brought the pets to work and installed a baby gate in the doorway to the back room so they could wander both inside and out in small, contained areas.

Bad idea with this many pets.

Prissy, my calico cat with an attitude befitting royalty, sauntered into the room first, her tail held high like a battle flag. Behind her came Wolfgang, Nik's Saint Bernard, whose size was matched only by his conviction that he was actually a lap dog. Willow, the Saint Berdoodle puppy we adopted from Jaz's poodles and Wolfgang's litter, bounced in next, her curly fur bobbing with each enthusiastic leap.

The final parade members were Jaz's full-sized poodle twins—Chanel, and Versace—and the puppy they kept from the litter, Armani, who was the biggest boy of the bunch. Willow was the runt. They scampered in like furry torpedoes, making a beeline for the couch where Aunt Tasoula had just unfurled the Aphrodite concept art.

"No, no, no!" I yelped, diving for the puppies, but I was too late.

Armani had already begun scaling the back of the couch, his big paws finding purchase in the fabric Jaz had just reupholstered last month, with Willow hot on his heels. Chanel and Versace, never ones to be out-done, formed what could only be described as a puppy blockade across the entrance to the fitting rooms.

"They're so cute," Jaz cooed, completely uncon-cerned by the catastrophe unfolding before us. "Oh! That reminds me—we need to discuss whether the pets will have roles in the ceremony. I'm thinking Wolfgang could be the ring bearer. We'd need to find him a big tuxedo, of course."

The image of Nik's one-hundred-and-seventy-pound dog trotting down the aisle with rings tied to his collar sent a fresh wave of panic through me. Be-fore I could articulate this, Wolfgang decided to show-case his grace by attempting to curl up beneath the display table holding my most delicate pieces.

The table wobbled ominously.

"Wolf, no!" I lunged just as Willow, excited by my sudden movement, leaped up to lick my face. The combination sent me gagging and stumbling back-ward into Ma, who dropped her handful of tulle-wrapped koufeta.

The tiny packages scattered across the floor like fancy marbles.

My phone buzzed again, this time with a text. I pulled it from my pocket to find a message from Nik.

Hope your morning's going well. Love you to the moon and back, future Mrs. Stevens.

For just a moment, the pandemonium receded. The simple message acted like a reset button, re-minding me why I was willingly subjecting myself to this matrimonial madness. For Nik. For us. For the life we were building together.

Then Prissy, apparently offended by not being the center of attention for a full thirty seconds, leaped onto the counter and deliberately—with the calculated malice only cats can truly master—swiped her paw at the box of wedding favor samples Jaz had just opened. The box tipped, its contents spilling across my careful displays in a cascade of tiny bells, miniature olive oil bottles, and custom-printed napkins.

The boutique fell silent as we all watched the last napkin flutter to the floor, landing with perfect irony so the words "Happily Ever After" faced upward.

I looked around at the mess—my ma with sugar-dusted hands, Jaz frozen in the act of catching a falling thank you card sample, Aunt Tasoula tangled in concept art, pets in various states of mischief—and felt a laugh bubble up from somewhere deep in my chest.

"Well," I said, bending to pick up a koufeta bag that had somehow remained intact, "I guess this is what they mean by 'for better or worse,' right?"

Aunt Tasoula beamed at me. "That the spirit, Kalliope! Now, about the centerpieces ..."

I lifted my hands and surrendered to the beautiful disaster that was my life.

Sunny

THE TAROT CARDS felt warm beneath my fingers, almost alive with possibility as I sat at the kitchen table at *Divine Inspiration*, the quaint inn my doctor father and lawyer mother had bought when they retired to be near us in Divinity, NY. I shuffled the cards, breathing in the buttery scent of Granny Gert's cookie dough as sunlight spilled through the curtains, painting golden patches across the worn wooden surface.

There was something in the air today—not just Great Grandma Tootsie singing showtunes or Fiona dancing or Granny humming—something electric, like the moment before lightning strikes. Granny made the cookies, Fiona made the pies, and Tootsie made everything else at the inn, calling themselves The Tasty Trio.

"Sunny, dear, pass the nutmeg, would you?" Granny Gert's flour-dusted hands kneaded the dough rhythmically, her wrists moving with surprising strength for a woman of eighty. Her snow-white hair from getting scarlet fever as a teenager was perfectly styled after being set and curled once a week since I could remember.

I slid the small jar across the counter without looking up from my cards. "Here you go, Granny." I'd always been closer to my grandmother than my mother, Vivian, but we had come a long way since I'd gotten married and had children of my own.

"Thank you, sweetie." Granny winked at me with her snappy brown eyes, a conspirator in the morning quiet.

She wore an old flour sack she'd made into an apron and kept her wooden spoon in the pocket. Her cookies she stored in an old pumpkin cookie jar with a foil wrapped plate for a lid, saying that was where the magic happened in making her cookies taste incredible.

Granny had a cookie for every occasion.

"Reading anything interesting in those cards of yours?" she asked.

I got my psychic abilities from my grandmother, though she'd never really developed hers. I used fortune-teller tools to aid in my readings, and tarot cards were the easiest tool to bring with me on the go. I always carried a deck with me when I traveled, which we were about to do. Before I could answer, Great-Grandma Tootsie's voice cut through the kitchen in her sing-song tone.

"Boys oh day, my hip is acting up again," she said, using one of her favorite, quirky sayings. "Mark my words, there's rain coming." She wasn't my biological great grandmother, but she was a great grandma to everyone at one hundred years old, and still about the best cook in the county.

No recipes needed ... just a little of this, a little of that, and a whole lot of love.

She adjusted herself in her chair by the window, since her services weren't needed today, humming showtunes. No music necessary there either, other than the notes filtering through her mind from days long ago. My snow-white cat, Morty, sat curled in her lap with a bowtie Granny Gert had made for him.

"The weather app says sunshine all day, Tootsie," Fiona chimed in, dancing as she dumped filling into her pie. She looked perfectly put together and dressed for a garden party, her hair still colored auburn even though she was eighty as well.

"Fiddlesticks. That phone of yours knows nothing about real forecasting." Tootsie tapped her cane against the floor for emphasis. "My hip hasn't been wrong yet." She went back to singing and bobbing her gray head.

I hid my smile with a sip of peppermint tea.

Across the kitchen, my three-year-old daughter Tina was conducting what appeared to be a serious investigation. Her short, dark hair like the daddy she idolized didn't move an inch as she crawled around her one-year-old brother River's highchair, an over-sized magnifying glass clutched in her tiny fist. The magnifying glass was a gift from my husband, Mitch, who clearly underestimated a toddler's ability to turn any object into a weapon.

"Whatcha doing there, Detective Tina?" I ask, arranging my cards in a neat stack.

Tina looked up at me with solemn gray eyes also like her daddy's. "I'm looking for clues, Mommy." Each word was carefully pronounced, as if she were explaining quantum physics to a particularly slow student.

"Clues about what?"

She pointed the magnifying glass at River, who was in dire need of a first haircut, but I couldn't bring myself to chop off his beautiful blond curls. He was happily smashing a banana between his pudgy fingers. "River's a suspect," she replied.

"A suspect in what case?"

"The Case of the Missing Cookies." Tina narrowed her eyes at her brother, who responded by offering her a squished piece of banana with a drool-covered grin, his green eyes full of the devil, like mine.

I bit back a laugh. The missing cookies were most definitely in Tootsie's sweater pocket—I'd spotted her sneaking them earlier—but I wouldn't blow her cover. Some mysteries were better left unsolved, especially when they involved Tootsie's sweet tooth.

Turning back to my cards, I closed my eyes and centered myself. The kitchen faded away—Granny Gert's singing, Tootsie's humming, Fiona's dancing, and Tina's detective monologue—until all I felt was the deck in my hands and the quiet pulse of energy flowing through me. I drew the first card and placed it face up on the table.

The Ten of Swords.

My stomach dropped. Ten swords piercing a

figure lying face down, a black sky above, blood staining the ground beneath. It wasn't the card you wanted to see on a Saturday morning before a second cup of tea.

"Well, that's not ideal," I muttered.

Granny Gert glanced over, flour dusting her cheek like pollen coating everything outside. "That bad, huh?"

I was about to respond when something shifted in the air around me. The kitchen blurred at the edges; sounds became muffled as if I were under water. My breath caught in my throat as the vision crashed into me without warning.

White lace. Flowers. The sweet scent of roses mixed with something metallic.

I saw Kalli, my friend from the cruise ship, standing in her wedding dress, radiant and laughing. But then the image twisted, darkening at the corners. Her wedding veil fluttered in a sudden breeze, and as it settled back down, I saw it—a splash of crimson spreading across a white piece of delicate fabric.

Red on white. Blood on lace. Could it be her veil?

Kalli's smile faltered, her eyes widening with confusion, and somewhere in the background, I heard screams.

The vision faded as quickly as it came, leaving me gasping at my kitchen table, my hands trembling above the Ten of Swords.

"Land sakes, child." Granny Gert's voice sounded far away. "You've gone white as my flour."

I blinked rapidly, trying to ground myself back in the present. The kitchen came into focus again: the warm yellow walls, the herb pots on the windowsill, the new curtains my mother had hung. *This* was reality.

The blood was just a vision.

"I saw something," I whispered, my voice unsteady. "About Kalli's wedding."

The kitchen door swung open, and Mitch walked in, bringing with him the scent of fresh air and coffee. He was dressed in his standard jeans and a sport coat with his gun and badge on his hips, his expression shifting from relaxed to concerned as he took in my face.

"Let me guess ... there's going to be a murder at the wedding?" he asked, his frown deepening as he set his coffee cup on the counter. He always had an uncanny ability to pick up on my thoughts, though he lacked my psychic abilities.

He was street smart.

"I'm not sure about murder, but the dream I had a while back and this newest vision confirm there will definitely be drama at the wedding," I said, as the image of the bloodied lace flashed in my mind again.

I'd first seen blood on lace in a vision when the guys were in Atlantic City. I had thought it was connected to that, but after he got home, I had another dream and thought it might be connected to Kalli's wedding. Now the vision included Kalli's wedding dress, so I was sure something dramatic was about to happen.

Mitch pulled out the chair across from me and sat down, his eyes serious. "They're Greek. I would expect nothing less. What did you see?"

Before I could answer, a high-pitched giggle erupted from River's highchair, followed by a collective gasp from everyone in the kitchen. River's plastic spoon was floating, suspended in mid-air about six inches above his tray. The baby clapped his hands in delight, his blond curls bouncing, and the spoon did a little twirl before dropping back down with a clatter.

"Well, I'll be," whispered Tootsie, suddenly forgetting all about her hip.

Tina's magnifying glass dropped from her hand. "River's magic!" she exclaimed with wide eyes.

Mitch ran a hand through his hair. "Well, that's new."

"He's stronger than I am," I said in awe, momentarily distracted from my vision by my son's display of power. While I'd always had visions and a connection to energy that manifested in fortune teller tools and occasional premonitions, River seemed to have inherited a more tangible form of our family's gift.

Apparently, he could move objects with his mind.

"What am *I*?" Tina demanded, putting her hands on her hips and sticking her bottom lip out.

"You, my sweet pea," said Granny Gert with a wink, "are one clever detective extraordinaire. That's *your* special power."

This seemed to satisfy Tina, who returned to her investigation with renewed vigor, though now she kept glancing at her brother warily.

"Back to the wedding," Mitch said, redirecting us. He'd always been uncomfortable with my ability and wasn't nearly ready to deal with his son's even stronger capabilities. "What exactly did you see, Sunny?"

I took a deep breath and described the vision—Kalli in her wedding dress, the lace, the blood. As I spoke, the kitchen grew quieter. Everyone, even Tootsie, leaned forward to catch every word.

"Could be symbolic," Granny Gert suggested. "Blood doesn't always mean actual blood, dearie."

"But with the Ten of Swords ..." I gestured to the card still lying ominously on my table in front of me.

Mitch's jaw tightened. "I'll be there anyway, as Nik's groomsman. I'll keep my eyes open, Tink." He'd always called me Tink, short for Tinkerbell, and I called him Detective Grumpy Pants, though these days he had softened considerably.

"We'll *all* be there, honey," I reminded him.

"The whole Divinity circus heading to Connecticut for the wedding," Tootsie cackled. "Boys oh day, I'm so happy those Greek mamas included us."

"Aren't they just the bee's knees?" Granny Gert put the cookies on a tray. "I just love weddings."

"They sure are something." Fiona put her pie in the oven. "I can't wait to dance at the reception."

Despite my lingering unease, I couldn't help but smile at the image. Our Tasty Trio wasn't all that different from the Three Act Mamas.

The wedding wasn't for a month, but the Greek mamas kept changing and adding things to the point that Kalli had sent me a 911 message, asking me to come early for a vacation and to bring reinforcements. So, we'd all made arrangements for our staff to run our businesses, and we were headed to Clearview today.

"Is everything packed?" Granny Gert asked, finally sliding her cookies into the oven. "The Tasty Trio will be ready to roll shortly."

"We're all packed, just waiting on Mom and Dad to come down," I answered.

"I forgot a few things back at our house," Mitch said, standing up. "I'll be back shortly."

I nodded, reaching over to wipe banana from River's cheek.

As Mitch left, I tried to shake off the lingering dread from my vision. Maybe Granny Gert was right. Maybe it was symbolic. Maybe the red was just wine spilled on Kalli's veil, or red roses, or anything other than what it looked like.

But the Ten of Swords lay there on my table, ten blades piercing a fallen figure, and I couldn't quite convince myself.

River giggled again, and this time it was my tarot deck that shifted, the cards fanning out in a perfect arc before settling back into a neat stack.

"Show-off," I said softly with a smile as my beautiful green-eyed, blond-haired boy beamed back at me, innocent and powerful and completely unaware of the storm I feared was coming.

2

KALLI

The morning air was crisp, carrying the scent of the season's first full bloom as I stepped onto the cobblestone walkway leading to the parish center for *Holy Trinity Greek Orthodox Church*. It was the perfect June morning—sunny, just warm enough to be pleasant, but not so hot that I'd regret wearing my pale blue linen dress. The only problem?

I was walking into a battlefield disguised as a wedding planning meeting.

Jaz was already there, standing at the entrance, phone in one hand and what looked like a three-foot-long to-do list in the other. Her caramel hair fell in waves over her shoulders, and her expression was one of pure determination.

"Oh good, you're here," she said, barely glancing up. "We're running behind schedule." She took her job as maid of honor seriously.

"We're not late," I pointed out, adjusting the strap of my purse on my shoulder.

She waved me off. "In wedding time, we're already behind."

I rolled my eyes and stepped inside. The main hall was bustling with movement. Sunlight streamed through the large arched windows, casting a golden glow on the tiled floor.

Vanessa Hayes, our wedding planner, stood in the center, her clipboard clutched tightly to her chest like a shield. Her hair was in its usual sleek auburn ponytail, but the stress lines on her forehead were more pronounced than normal. She was juggling various tasks, her eyes darting from one corner of the room to the other.

"Kalli!" she called, relief evident in her voice as she spotted me. "We need to talk about the floral arrangements for the church and reception. The church's supplier had a mix-up, and instead of white peonies, we're getting blush roses."

I sighed, trying to maintain a calm demeanor. "That's not terrible."

Jaz scoffed. "It's not ideal, either."

Before I could respond, Ma and Aunt Tasoula swept in like a whirlwind, their voices already rising in debate. Chloe followed closely behind, her arms laden with sample decorations. Everyone seemed to want a say in planning my wedding.

"Roses classic," Ma announced, her tone leaving little room for argument.

"Peonies more elegant," Aunt Tasoula countered, her hands gesturing animatedly.

Chloe waved a hand dismissively. "As long as altar arrangements no clash with bridesmaids' dresses, who cares?"

I rubbed my temples. "It's fine. Blush roses will work." I was using Ma's friend, Wendy, for my bouquet and bridesmaids' flowers.

Vanessa sighed in relief. "Thank you, Kalli. I'll confirm the order. Wendy will be by later to confirm the rest."

From across the room, Barry Franklin, the DJ, was testing sound equipment, his frown deepening as he adjusted the knobs, muttering about feedback issues. He ran a hand over his bald head, then pushed his glasses up his nose. His assistant, a lanky teenager named Josh, was nervously holding a bundle of cables.

Nearby, Damon Lowe, the photographer, was busy checking the lighting and snapping test shots. He was a perfectionist in the way he dressed—designer jeans, trendy shirt, dark blond hair styled in the latest fashion—and it showed in the way he meticulously adjusted his camera settings.

"Damon," Vanessa called, "make sure you get some practice angles for Kalli's entrance into the church as well."

Damon looked up from his camera, his face lighting up with a confident smile. "Oh, don't worry. I plan on making her look flawless—even if I have to airbrush some stress wrinkles."

I raised a brow but didn't say anything.

Jaz narrowed her eyes at him. "You might want to fix your attitude ... I bite."

Angela Reynolds, the short, curvy seamstress, arrived just in time to catch that exchange. She gave me a knowing smirk before pushing her rolling sewing kit near a table. "I see things are moving smoothly," she said dryly, her eyes twinkling with amusement as she shook her light brown curls.

"As smoothly as a runaway chariot," I muttered, earning a chuckle from her.

Angela unrolled a piece of lace, inspecting the delicate beadwork. "I brought the final adjustments for your veil. You might want to check it before I do the last stitch."

I nodded, appreciating that she, at least, was handling things with some level of professionalism.

Next, Wendy Brooks arrived carrying two test arrangements, her soft smile a welcome contrast to the stress floating in the air. She was in her fifties and widowed, letting her shoulder length hair go natural gray. A regular at *Aphrodite's*, Ma had made her an honorary member of her weekly Biriba club, which Wendy found highly entertaining.

"I brought both bouquet options for you to see in person," she said, her voice gentle and reassuring. "One has more greenery, and the other focuses on the blush roses."

I took a deep breath. "You are a lifesaver, Wendy."

"Don't say that until you pick," she teased lightly, setting the arrangements down on a nearby table.

Troy Bennett, Damon's assistant, hovered nearby, shifting nervously as he adjusted a lighting fixture. He was tall and thin, with dark red hair and freckles, currently sweating even though the temperature in the hall was perfectly comfortable.

"Everything okay, Troy?" I asked, watching him closely as I touched his arm.

He nodded too quickly. "Yeah, just making sure the setup is perfect." *I can't afford for anything else to go wrong.*

I let go of his arm, feeling guilty for listening to his thoughts without cause. "I'm sure everything will be just fine."

Jaz arched an eyebrow at him as he wiped sweat off his brow, but she said nothing, turning her attention back to Vanessa.

Meanwhile, Marcus Eldridge—the real estate developer funding the parish center renovations after the recent snake infestation nearly destroyed the church—sauntered in, dressed in his usual crisp black suit. He had salt and pepper hair, was stocky, and had the air of a man who wanted people to notice him.

"This is looking ... acceptable, I guess," Marcus commented, scanning the hall with a critical eye.

"Acceptable?" I repeated, narrowing my gaze.

"For an event of this scale," he amended smoothly. "Both you and your fiancé's families are quite large and make up half the town. I just hope the logistics don't fall apart at the last minute. It would be ... unfortunate."

Jaz rolled her eyes and muttered under her breath, "Wow, so reassuring."

I exhaled slowly. Between the vendors, our overzealous families, and the growing tension surrounding certain members of our planning committee, this wedding might be more complicated than I'd expected.

Eloping was sounding better by the minute.

Sunny

THE DRIVE FROM DIVINITY, New York to Clearview, Connecticut should have been peaceful. Instead, it felt like a circus on wheels.

Mitch was at the wheel, his fingers drumming against the dash in a steady rhythm to classic rock music. Next to him, Granny Gert and Great Grandma Tootsie were in the middle of a heated debate about whether or not it was appropriate to bring a "just in case" casserole to a wedding week.

"It's practical!" Granny Gert insisted. "What if the food isn't good?"

"It's a Greek wedding," I interjected from the back seat. "I'm sure the food will be incredible."

Tootsie hummed, stopping long enough to add, "Doesn't mean we shouldn't have a backup."

Mitch turned the music up.

Meanwhile, in the car seat next to me, River let out a delighted squeal and made his stuffed hound dog levitate above his head.

Tina, ever the observant detective-in-training, gasped. "River! That's against the rules!" she scolded.

River just giggled, clapping his chubby hands as the hound dog did a slow spin in the air.

Mitch sighed. "Sunny, can you—"

"I got it." I reached over and gently placed a hand on River's. "Not now, buddy. We have to be careful."

He pouted but let the stuffed dog drop into his lap.

I turned my attention back to the tarot deck in my lap. I'd drawn another card before we left. The Tower. A card of upheaval and chaos. Something was going to happen soon. I had a feeling Kalli's wedding was about to get a lot more complicated.

By the time we arrived at the *Clearview Hotel*, the parking lot was already packed. Kalli had said the summer solstice festival brought in a lot of out-of-town guests. The moment we stepped into the lobby, we were met with a familiar sight—Cole and Jo, wrangling their energetic four-year-old twin boys, Collin and Jeremiah. Collin looked just like Cole and Jeremiah took after Jo.

"Uncle Mitch! Aunt Sunny!" the boys shouted in unison, charging forward.

Tina scowled. "Ewww boys."

Mitch crouched just in time to scoop one up while the other clung to my leg.

Jo, looking every bit the fierce redheaded Amazon

she was, shook her head. "They've been cooped up in the car too long. They need to burn energy."

Cole, towering like a friendly sasquatch, chuckled. "That, and they inherited Jo's competitive streak. Everything gets turned into a competition."

"Darn right," Jo muttered.

Before we could respond, Sean and Zoe arrived. Sean carried a diaper bag over one shoulder while Zoe held their newborn baby girl, Alannah, with her strawberry-blonde peach fuzz hair against her chest. The little preemie had surprised everyone by making an appearance over a month early.

"Just in time," Sean said, flashing his trademark dimpled grin. "Looks like we made it before the real madness starts."

Zoe, exhausted but happy, rocked the baby gently. "Please tell me there's decent coffee in this hotel."

Granny Gert looped an arm through Zoe's. "Forget coffee. You need one of my famous cookies."

Great Grandma Tootsie cooed to the baby. "And maybe a nap. That baby's barely a month old."

I smiled at them all, warmth settling in my chest. Family and friends. It didn't get any better than that. We checked in and headed to our rooms to get ready for the welcome event later that evening.

BY THE TIME we arrived at *Aphrodite's*, the evening air was thick with the scent of oregano, garlic, and sizzling lamb. Inside, the restaurant buzzed with laughter, the clinking of glasses, and the warm hum of Greek music floating through the air.

The Greek mamas were in full force, fluttering from table to table, ensuring everyone was fed and comfortable. Kalli's pop was behind the bar, pouring ouzo with her papou, while her yiayia sat at the head of the largest table, regal as ever, overseeing the gathering like a queen surveying her court.

I'd met them all when they'd descended on Divinity to help Kalli clear her name from a murder investigation when she'd come to visit me a while back.

Kalli's cousin, Frona, who had fallen off the apple wagon years ago and had never been the same, was her parents' dishwasher. She was happy but a handful, and I had witnessed that firsthand at my parents' inn. Currently, she kept coming out of the kitchen, her pig tails swinging as she skipped and cleared people's plates before they were finished, disappearing to do more dishes. She was obsessed with running the dishwasher even when it was empty.

Captain Crenshaw, who was engaged to Nik's ma, and Tate Hemsworth, who dated Kalli's Aunt Tasoula, sat at a long table up front with my parents, the Tasty Trio, and the babies. My head spun with how many people there were to keep track of, but with two big Greek families and my own crazy crew, things were bound to get interesting.

Meanwhile Mitch and I sat with Cole, Jo, Sean, Zoe, Nik, and Kalli at a back table, where the conversation had taken a decidedly nostalgic turn.

"So," Sean's mouth twisted into a lopsided grin as he leaned back in his chair, "let's talk about our wild time in Atlantic City. Anyone care to relive that?"

Boomer groaned, rubbing his face. "Can we not?"

Cole chuckled. "Oh, I think we must. That was one epic trip."

Jaz, standing nearby, crossed her arms. "Yes, let's discuss how my husband got tangled in some 'unfinished business.'" Her eyes locked onto Boomer's with the precision of a sniper ready to pull the trigger. She wasn't about to let them live this down.

Boomer sighed. "It wasn't—"

"Unfinished business?" Nik cut in, watching Boomer carefully. "That's a phrase that makes a cop nervous. I thought we were done with all that?"

Mitch's expression darkened.

Boomer hesitated. The laughter around the table faded slightly as an uneasy tension settled between them.

Nik's voice dropped an octave. "This have to do with Ferraro?" The moment the name left his lips, the energy in the room shifted.

Mitch stiffened beside me, his jaw tightening. The dim lighting couldn't hide the way his hands clenched into fists on the table. I reached under the table and placed a hand on his knee, squeezing gently.

"Wait," Cole said, frowning. "As in *Dominic Ferraro, the mobster who wanted to kill us*? He doesn't know where you live, does he?"

Boomer exhaled slowly. "It's nothing to worry about."

"It better not be." Jaz frowned. "You promised me he wouldn't be an issue."

"He's not," Boomer quickly added.

I didn't need to use my psychic abilities to know that was a lie.

"Boomer," I said carefully, keeping my voice light but firm. "That name carries weight. And not the good kind. Remember my visions from the bachelor party weekend? I'm seeing Kalli in those visions now."

He looked away, his fingers drumming lightly against the tabletop. "I made some calls. People are watching him. It's handled. He's nowhere near Clearview."

Mitch scoffed, finally speaking. "Do you have new information we don't know about, Boomer? If it's handled, we wouldn't be talking about it."

Kalli came back to the table with a drink. "Talking about what?"

"Wedding details. Nothing to worry about, Ballas," Nik said, no more words were necessary.

The group fell silent, the clinking of glasses and background chatter suddenly too distant. I cast a glance around the restaurant, feeling the familiar tingle of my intuition nudging me. Ferraro's name wasn't just something Boomer wanted to forget ... my gut said he knew more than he was letting on, and it was something we needed to worry about.

And I always listened to my gut.

3

KALLI

The moment I slipped into my mother's wedding dress, I felt the weight of tradition settle over me. The lace sleeves had been removed, the bodice altered to fit my frame, and the once-voluminous skirt had been streamlined into something simpler, more modern.

More *me*.

Even with all the changes, it still carried the history of my family. My ma's laughter. My pop's devotion. The countless times my yiayia had told me that love was about finding the person who saw all your flaws and still thought you were perfect.

I turned to face the full-length mirror in *Full Disclosure*, my fingers smoothing over the delicate beading at my waist. The ivory fabric glowed under the soft lighting, the details of the embroidery catching the shimmer of the chandelier above.

The shop was quiet, closed after hours for this fitting, with just me and my maid of honor, ensuring it would be peaceful. I needed peaceful right now. Even all our pets were at daycare so we would have no interruptions. Besides, I wanted the mamas to be surprised when they saw me walk down the aisle.

Angela stood behind me, pins tucked into the corner of her mouth as she made a few final adjustments to the hem. "It's coming together beautifully," she murmured around the pins, then plucked them out to speak clearly. "Just a few more tweaks, and it'll be perfect."

Jaz, standing off to the side, arms crossed, nodded in approval. "I gotta admit, I didn't think a vintage dress could look this good, but it's working. It's going to look great in the pictures Damon takes."

"I told you," I said, adjusting the neckline slightly until it fit perfectly. "I wanted something meaningful."

Angela snorted, tugging at the fabric as she pinned a new hemline. "Meaningful is great, but I swear, if I hear Damon Lowe's name one more time, I might start throwing sewing needles."

I turned slightly, meeting her gaze in the mirror. "Damon?"

Angela scoffed, shaking her head. "That man did everything he could to ruin my reputation. Spread rumors that I botched a high-profile designer collaboration. I lost work because of him."

I frowned. "I didn't know that."

"Oh, he was good at playing innocent," Angela muttered, tightening a few stitches, her face hardening. "But trust me, he has dirt on everyone. Holds it over their heads like some kind of power trip."

Jaz's eyes darkened. "Sounds like someone who has a lot of enemies."

Angela let out a sharp breath but didn't argue. "I wasn't the only one he burned," she admitted. "A lot of people have been waiting for karma to catch up with him."

Before I could respond, the bell above the boutique's door jingled, and Wendy stepped inside carrying a few bouquet samples. Wendy was a breath of fresh air, as always, her soft smile a soothing contrast to the pandemonium that surrounded wedding planning.

"I brought more options," she announced cheerfully, setting them on the counter. "Something classic, something modern, and something in between."

"You are an angel," I said sincerely, already moving toward the arrangements.

Wendy chuckled, brushing her gray-streaked hair out of her face. "Just someone who's seen enough brides melt down to know that flowers can solve a lot of problems."

She set the bouquets down on the shop's glass counter, carefully unwrapping each one. The classic arrangement was an elegant mix of white roses and eucalyptus. The modern one had a bolder touch with deep burgundy dahlias, and the in-between option blended soft pink peonies with subtle wildflowers for a more natural, romantic look.

I reached toward the peonies, drawn to the delicate contrast of color and texture, but just as my fingers brushed the petals, a sharp sneeze shattered my moment of calm. "Oh no," I whispered, already recoiling.

Angela, standing off to the side, sniffled, her eyes watering. "Sorry, allergies," she said, reaching for a tissue—and, to my absolute horror, brushing her fingers against a silk gown hanging on the rack beside her.

Jaz winced as I inhaled sharply, my hands instantly retreating from the bouquets as if the germs had leaped into the air, ready to attack.

"May the gods bless you, Angela," I managed

through clenched teeth. "Do you need—uh, some hand sanitizer?"

Angela, utterly oblivious to my rising panic, dabbed at her nose with a tissue. "I'm fine, thanks."

Jaz groaned. "Oh, for the love of—Kalli, breathe."

I sucked in a breath, stepping back from the flowers entirely. My mind was already racing through the ways to disinfect the area without coming across as completely insane.

Wendy, ever the peacemaker, smoothly pulled a small bottle of hand sanitizer from her tote and handed it to Angela. "Just in case, dear."

Angela took it with a grateful nod, using a small amount before handing the bottle back. "Better?" she asked, looking at me expectantly as she scrubbed her hands.

I gave her a sheepish smile. "Much."

"How ever are you going to handle your wedding reception?" Angela asked. "Have you seen how much hugging happens at Greek weddings?"

Jaz laughed. "Right? The amount of cheek-kissing alone is enough to send her into a panic."

"I've seen it, and I've *lived* it my entire life." I could feel my face pale. "Yet I'm *still* working on it."

Wendy smiled sympathetically. "At least you know everything else is under control. The church flowers are set, the reception centerpieces will be delivered on time, and the mamas have officially declared themselves satisfied with the arrangement of the floor plan for all of the surprises they want to set up."

Jaz made a face. "Satisfied for now. Give it another day."

I sighed, running my hands down the bodice of my dress, trying to shake the lingering stress. "I just want everything to be perfect."

Angela patted my shoulder lightly. *Nothing is ever perfect*, she thought, but said, "It will be. And if it isn't, no one will know the difference except you." Her hand fell away.

I knew she was right, but that didn't stop the panic that something was going to go very wrong from sticking in my gut.

It was then that I remembered my ma's advice about handling stress: *focus on big picture, Kalliope. You let go small details.* I took a deep breath, reminding myself that the wedding was about celebrating love and the union of two families. Wendy was right. Even if something went wrong, it wouldn't overshadow the joy of the day.

As we continued our preparations, Jaz and Wendy discussed the logistics of transporting the flowers to the church. Angela shared stories of brides she had worked with in the past, some of whom had faced far worse disasters than a sneeze-induced panic attack.

"Remember the bride whose dress caught fire?" Angela said with a chuckle, shaking her head. "Now that was a real emergency. We managed to save the dress, and the wedding went on without a hitch."

There was nothing that happened in Clearview that remained a secret.

Jaz laughed. "Oh, I remember that. And the one who lost her ring just minutes before the ceremony."

Wendy looked off, and her eyes grew misty. "Weddings are always full of surprising twists, but they always turn out beautifully in the end. I'll remember mine until the day I die." She blinked back tears and nodded. "It's all about how you handle the unexpected."

Her words were comforting, and I found myself relaxing a bit more. The dress fitting continued smoothly, and by the time we were finished, I felt much more confident about the upcoming wedding.

As I left the boutique, I carried with me a renewed sense of calm and a determination to focus on the joy of the day rather than the potential mishaps. This wedding was going to be a celebration of love and life, and nothing was going to take that away from us.

Sunny

KALLI AND JAZ were so busy with wedding planning, that I'd offered up my family to help. Zoe and Jo were watching the kids because the Tasty Trio had insisted on coming along, even though I suspected that would be more of a hindrance than a help.

I sighed. They meant well ... *most* of the time.

Vanessa met us at the entrance of the parish center, her clipboard clutched tightly against her chest as if it might shield her from the stress of wedding planning. Her normally pristine posture was slightly hunched, and her expression strained.

The pressure of the wedding—or something else —was clearly getting to her.

Her fingers tapped anxiously against the edge of the clipboard, and the tightness in her jaw suggested she was barely holding it together. Her auburn hair, usually sleek and perfectly styled, had a few stray wisps that had escaped from her bun, and the light sheen of sweat on her forehead betrayed her exhaustion.

"Effie said you could store the gifts in the back closet," she stated, already turning down the hallway before we could reply. Her heels clicked against the polished floors, the sharp, rushed rhythm mirroring her tension. "I'll unlock it for you."

My mom trailed behind me, balancing a neatly wrapped package on one arm while adjusting the strap of her purse with the other. My dad held a small crate of liquor bottles, his brow furrowed in disapproval as he glanced down at the labels.

"I still say the catering could use a bit more refinement," Dad muttered, his voice carrying more than necessary in the otherwise quiet hall. "Ouzo is fine, but where's the aged scotch, Vivian?"

Mom rolled her eyes, barely concealing her exasperation. "Donald, it's a Greek wedding, not a whiskey tasting. And Kalli is not our daughter."

"Oh, boys oh day, I like whiskey," Great Grandma Tootsie said. "Rye and ginger is my favorite cocktail. It's the secret to my longevity." She winked, then started humming.

"I prefer wine," Fiona said, twirling in a circle. "Fruity, crisp, and light as a feather ... just like me."

"You're fruity all right." Granny Gert snickered. "I say fiddlesticks to the scotch and wine. I'll take a good cocktail any day. Who's gonna notice if I spike the wedding punch with a little extra love?" Her snappy brown eyes sparkled.

I groaned, already knowing where this was going. "Ladies, no."

Granny Gert shot me an innocent look, which was anything but. "What? Weddings are supposed to be lively. Nothing livens up a party like a well-timed 'secret ingredient.' Right girls?"

Fiona and Great Grandma Tootsie nodded a little too enthusiastically.

"That family is lively enough," Mom scoffed, slipping past Dad to be first in line at the closet. "If you try anything, Mother, I'm making sure you sit next to Kalli's mother, Ophelia, during the reception. She'll talk your ear off about the benefits of aloe and Duct tape, and why she thinks meditation is a scam."

Granny Gert paled. "You wouldn't."

"Try me." My mom looked at the other two members of the Tasty Trio. "And don't think I won't find the perfect spots for you both as well. Kalli's aunt Tasoula would just love to get her hands on Fiona's hair and makeup."

Fiona gasped. "What's wrong with the way I look?"

"Trust me, you don't want to find out what Tasoula thinks. She's very persuasive and will have you in her chair before you can say, 'Opa!'" My mother looked at Tootsie. "And don't think you're immune just because you're one hundred years old, Toots. Nik's mother, Chloe, will be sure to give you a little extra Greek TLC. You can bet she'll help you to your seat, make sure you don't eat anything bad for you, and you can forget about that rye and ginger."

"Well, I'll be. I can take care of myself. Been doing it for a century." Toots stood as straight as her arthritic back would allow.

"Tell that to a Greek mama." My mother narrowed her eyes. "So, are we all clear on behaving ourselves at this wedding?"

Vanessa sighed heavily before they could answer, the weight of our family's banter seemingly pressing down on her already frayed nerves. "Alright," she said, fishing out a key and fumbling slightly before unlocking a closet door. "Just set everything in here, and we'll sort it later."

The closet was larger than I expected, filled with neatly stacked chairs, folded tablecloths, and extra linens. A few small boxes were already tucked into the corner—decorations waiting to be arranged for the wedding reception. The faint scent of lavender and old wood filled the air as I stepped inside, my mother following close behind to arrange the gifts on the lowest shelf.

"Be careful with that one, Sunny," Mom warned, nodding toward a particularly delicate-looking package as I moved it aside to make room.

"I got it," I assured her, carefully shifting the box. As I reached to adjust a particularly heavy one, my fingers accidentally brushed against Vanessa's planner.

A sudden, sharp vision flooded my mind.

A dimly lit room. The flickering glow of a flame. Paper curling and blackening at the edges, smoke rising in delicate wisps. Vanessa's trembling hands tossing something into the fire, her breath uneven. The acrid scent of burning ink filled my senses, the edges of her fingers shaking as she watched the paper dissolve into ash.

The heat from the flames felt real, my lungs tightening as if the smoke were suffocating me. The shadows in the vision danced wildly, the firelight illuminating Vanessa's tear-streaked face. Her lips moved, murmuring something frantic, but the words were lost in the crackling of the burning paper.

She hesitated, her fingers hovering over the last remaining scraps of paper, a deep hesitation evident in her tense shoulders. But then, with one final, shaky breath, she shoved the rest of the paper into the fire, watching as the embers consumed every last scrap.

Then—darkness.

The vision snapped away so quickly that I staggered slightly, gripping the edge of a shelf to steady myself. My pulse pounded in my ears, the lingering scent of smoke almost tangible. A cold sweat prickled at the back of my neck.

Vanessa stared at me, her brow furrowed. "Something wrong?"

I blinked, shaking off the remnants of the vision as best as I could. The logical part of my brain told me to press for answers, to question her about what I had just seen. But the guarded look in her eyes, the way she tightened her grip on her planner, told me I wouldn't get anything out of her now.

"I—" My voice faltered, but I forced a smile, even as my stomach churned. "No. Nothing at all."

Vanessa hesitated for half a second, then nodded briskly, turning back to the doorway. "Alright, well, if you need anything else, I'll be finishing up some last-minute arrangements in the church."

Mom, who had been busy adjusting some ribbons on the gift table, glanced up. "Vanessa, darling, are you alright? You look pale."

Vanessa's eyes widened slightly before she quickly waved a hand. "Oh, I'm fine! Just a lot on my plate."

Granny Gert tsked. "Stress will do that to you, dearie. Maybe you should sit down, have a cookie." She held out the tray she'd brought for the church.

"Or a piece of pie." Fiona stepped forward.

"I'm sure I could find some rye around here." Tootsie winked.

Mom just shook her head at all of them. Clearly, they didn't plan to behave one bit.

Vanessa let out a weak laugh, then quickly excused herself, fleeing down the hallway. I watched her go, my mind racing with possibilities. What had she burned? A letter? A contract? A confession?

Deep down, I knew Vanessa was hiding something. And whatever it was, it terrified her.

And now, it terrified me too.

4

KALLI

Sinfully Delicious smelled like Mount Olympus had showered the bakery in sugar, cinnamon, and a sprinkling of roasted almonds. The warm scent of pastries mingled with the luscious aroma of buttercream frosting. I was more into health food, but Nik loved sugar, and our wedding cake was as much for our guests as it was for us.

I stepped inside with Ma, Chloe, and my ever-opinionated Maid of Honor, Jaz.

The bakery was buzzing with activity, the glass display cases filled to the brim with cakes, cookies, pastries, and baklava, all glistening under the soft, golden light. A line of eager customers stood at the counter, some cradling boxes tied with pastel ribbons, others debating the array of sugary delights. The walls were lined with photos of extravagant wedding cakes— each more elaborate than the last—making my head spin just thinking about all the options.

"I say baklava tower most elegant," Ma declared, waving her hand like she was announcing a royal decree. "It tradition. It Greek. It masterpiece of honey-soaked perfection. Enough said."

Chloe scoffed, her arms crossed over her designer

blazer. "A five-tier gold-and-white masterpiece far more suitable. It grand. It sophisticated. It look incredible in pictures."

Thank Zeus Aunt Tasoula wasn't here.

Jaz snorted, rolling her eyes. "Kalli, tell them you don't want either of those. We talked about this. Clean lines, minimalist, a simple, modern cake that actually tastes good—not something that looks like a Vegas attraction or a Greek mythology exhibit."

I rubbed my temples, struggling to stay calm. "I just want something classic and elegant—without causing an international incident between our families." Every week, the mamas tried to make me change my mind or add new things. I was so confused on what ideas were even mine anymore.

The baker, a petite woman named Irene, smiled patiently from behind the counter. Maria, the owner, had hired her, saying she was the best in town, and her reputation regarding her wedding cakes was well-deserved.

"Luckily, we have plenty of options for you to try before making a decision," she intervened as if she'd been in this predicament countless times before. "Why don't we start with the tastings?"

A server brought out a platter of cake samples—with a separate smaller platter just for me—each slice meticulously decorated and ready to be devoured. The Greek mamas pounced, armed with tiny forks and formidable opinions, eating off each other's plates.

I had to look away and focus on my *sanitary* plate while taking deep breaths.

Chloe took a bite of a decadent chocolate cake, nodding with approval, while Ma sampled a honey and almond sponge, muttering about the importance of tradition. Jaz and I sampled the vanilla-bean buttercream in unison, exchanging a knowing glance as we did. Just as I was about to take a second bite, the door chimed.

Damon Lowe swaggered in, a camera slung over his shoulder and an infuriating smirk on his face. His presence alone sucked the lightness from the room, and I clenched my jaw as he made his way toward us, snapping a photo of me with my mouth open before I could even react.

The mamas insisted on him as our wedding photographer because he was the best, but he never listened to my wishes.

"Ah, nothing like a bride-to-be tasting cake," he mused, lowering his camera just slightly. "Gotta capture the moment. The stress, the indecision," he paused a beat, "the inevitable bridezilla meltdown." Then snapped more pictures as I gasped.

Jaz glared at him. "Put the camera away, Damon, or I swear I'll shove that lens somewhere very unpleasant."

Irene cleared her throat politely. "Perhaps we should focus on the cakes?"

Damon chuckled but lowered his camera. "Just doing my job, ladies. You know, capturing memories." His eyes flicked to a man who had just walked in behind him—Marcus Eldridge.

The atmosphere in the room shifted immediately. The real estate developer's usually polished demeanor looked slightly rumpled today, and he wasn't here for cake. He and Damon exchanged a look filled with enough tension to slice through fondant.

Marcus bumped my shoulder as he brushed past us, heading toward the counter. *He's going to push the wrong person too far someday.*

I wasn't sure if it was a warning or a prophecy, but it sent an uneasy shiver down my spine.

The tension in the room thickened as Marcus ordered an espresso, his gaze lingering on Damon as if contemplating something far beyond coffee choices. Damon's expression was smug, but he said nothing, his fingers drumming lazily against the side of his camera.

I shot Jaz a look, and she raised an eyebrow in silent agreement—something was definitely off here.

"Alright, enough distractions. Time's a wasting," Irene announced brightly, trying to cut through the palpable tension. "Let's move on to our next selection: a lemon chiffon with raspberry filling."

I tried to focus on the task at hand, but my mind kept wandering back to the exchange between Marcus and Damon. The cake tasting continued, with the Greek mamas arguing over every flavor, while Jaz was taking detailed notes and making funny comments trying to keep me sane.

Marcus took his espresso to a corner table, his eyes never leaving Damon. Every now and then, Damon would glance over his shoulder, his smug expression faltering just a bit. The whole scene felt like a powder keg ready to explode.

As we wrapped up the tasting, Irene handed me a card with her recommendations, our fingers brushing. *Good luck to this one. She's gonna need it with these matriarchs.*

I thanked her, trying to muster as much enthusiasm as I could, but I was in agreement. The mamas were driving me insane. She walked off with the mamas still hot on her heels, giving her more unsolicited advice on what she could do to make the cake even better.

The woman had the patience of a saint.

Damon had finally left, but Marcus remained, his espresso untouched. He sat there with his gaze still locked on the door as if waiting for something—or someone.

Jaz and I stepped outside, the bakery's drama left behind.

She nudged me, her eyes troubled. "You know, the cake is going to be amazing, but it looks like the real fireworks might happen before the wedding."

I groaned. "My thoughts exactly. Let's just hope they fizzle out before I walk down the aisle."

"Amen, sister." Jaz linked arms with me. "Come on, let's go find something to distract you before you start worrying about the next crisis."

As we walked away, I couldn't help but glance back at the bakery, feeling like we had just stepped out of a scene in a mystery novel. My mind raced with thoughts, wondering about the next steps to take. It seemed that our wedding was becoming more complicated each day. I turned to Jaz, who had always been the voice of reason.

"Jaz, what do you think about all this? I feel like things are getting out of control. It doesn't even feel like my wedding anymore."

Jaz sighed, her eyes reflecting the concern in her voice. "Kalli, you know weddings bring out the best and the worst in people. We just need to stay focused on what's important—your happiness and the joy of marrying Nik. Everything else is just noise."

I nodded, appreciating her advice. "You're right. It's just ... I never imagined the planning part would be this stressful."

"Remember mine? Don't worry. I've got you just

like you had me." Jaz squeezed my arm reassuringly. "Now, let's go find something fun to do."

"That's exactly what we need. Some fun. Just you and me. Let's make it happen." All I wanted was for Nik's and my wedding to be simple, filled with love, laughter, and unforgettable moments. That should be easy ...

So why did it feel like climbing Mount Olympus to make it happen?

Sunny

Diner Delights was packed, as expected. Kalli's cousins, Kosmos and Silas, owned the place, and their diner was a staple in Clearview, serving up the best gyros and soumada in town. Kalli had told me the traditional almond-based cold drink was a big favorite, and on any other day, I'd be eyeing the dessert section, but not today.

The scent of sizzling meats and freshly brewed coffee filled the air as I slid into a booth next to Mitch, with Boomer and Nik across from us. The retro-style diner buzzed with conversation, the occasional clang of silverware against plates punctuating the hum of voices. Waitresses weaved between tables, clearing plates and refilling coffee cups. A jukebox in the corner played an old Elvis tune, barely audible over the chatter and the sizzle of the grill.

Boomer had called the meeting, insisting the women get left behind. That alone set my nerves on edge. When he explained it was official police business, Mitch offered up my services since I often consulted with the police back in Divinity. And since I had recently had visions that pertained to Clearview, Boomer had agreed. He stirred his coffee absentmindedly, staring into the dark liquid like it held the answers to all life's problems.

When he finally spoke, his voice was low but firm. "Ferraro's men have been snooping around."

"I thought someone had eyes on him?" Nik's jaw unhinged, his fingers drumming against the table. "Where did you see his men?"

"Downtown. Last night and again this morning." Boomer looked up, his eyes serious. "Sorry, man. I really didn't expect to see them in Clearview. He must have slipped by the FBI's radar. I'll make another call."

Nik's jaw tensed. "This is Kalli's wedding month, and our town. Forget the FBI. We're locking this down after the wedding. Can we just try to get through that first?" His voice was firm, but even he couldn't hide the worry creeping in. "I promised her nothing would mess this up."

Mitch gave Boomer a hard look. "You sure they don't already know something? If they think you still have that drive—"

Boomer shook his head, cutting him off. "You guys know I don't have it, but they think I do, because they couldn't find it on Anthony 'the shark' Carbone after we left Atlantic City. And Ginger Debois, the redheaded grifter who worked with them both, has disappeared." Boomer swallowed hard. "They took him out in his own home. I don't know how they found out where I live. I keep everything unlisted for a reason." He rubbed the back of his neck. I hadn't known him long, but he looked more stressed than I'd ever seen him. "I don't want this spilling over into the wedding. Kalli deserves better."

The weight of his words settled over the table, thick and unspoken.

Kosmos appeared just in time, balancing a tray of food and setting down plates piled high with fries, club sandwiches, and Boomer's double bacon cheeseburger.

"Eat," Kosmos instructed, his voice gruff. "Looks like you all could use it." He gave us a knowing look before heading back to the kitchen.

Boomer sighed but picked up his burger anyway. "I just want to get through this wedding without a crime scene. I don't need another event ruined by my past."

Nik grunted. "Now that's wishful thinking."

Mitch chewed on a fry, his gaze flicking among us. "We need to stay ahead of them. If Ferraro's guys are watching you, they're watching all of us. I'm sure he still wants payback for his girlfriend dying in the crossfire during your undercover sting operation that went south." He glanced at the diner door, as if expecting trouble to walk in at any moment.

Boomer cursed under his breath. "I know. That's why I've been lying low. I don't want anything messing up Nik and Kalli's big day." He took a huge bite of his burger, like it might be his last meal.

I looked at all of them. "I'm worried my visions are coming true." I sighed, shaking my head. "Maybe after the wedding you guys can actually focus on something normal for a change—like visiting each other without having to solve a crime."

Nik grunted. "I don't know if I remember how to do that." He shoved a handful of fries into his mouth, trying to appear more relaxed than he actually was.

Boomer wiped ketchup off his chin. "So much for your vacation." He looked at Mitch. "Maybe we should all take a real vacation after this. You know, someplace with zero murder. Think that exists?"

Mitch snorted. "Doubtful. Nik and I met on vacation and look how that turned out." He was trying to act casual, but his eyes never stopped scanning the diner.

Just then, the bell above the door jingled.

A man in a jean jacket stepped inside, pausing near the entrance. He didn't sit. Didn't order. Instead, his gaze swept across the room, assessing every table like he was looking for someone specific.

The noise carried on around us—conversations, the clang of plates, the occasional burst of laughter—but my focus narrowed in on him. Something was off. My stomach twisted with unease. I couldn't read minds like Kalli, but my psychic abilities sent a distinct warning through my gut—this guy wasn't here for the milkshakes.

Mitch followed my gaze and tensed beside me, his grip tightening on his coffee cup.

Boomer sighed, setting his burger down. "Looks like the fun never stops."

The man spotted Boomer, locked eyes with him for a long moment. No words were exchanged, but the silent message was clear: I see you. Then, just as casually as he had entered, the man turned and walked out.

Nik watched him go; his expression unreadable. "We need to stay alert."

Mitch set his coffee down with a thud. "Agreed."

I swallowed hard, the foreboding settling deep in my chest. There was going to be a showdown at some point, and it wasn't going to be good. "We should tell Kalli and Jaz that Ferraro is in town. They'll be upset, and rightfully so, if we keep them out of the loop."

Nik shook his head, his mouth set in a grim line. "They're not the police. Kalli's got enough on her plate with the wedding prep. Let her enjoy this month. The last thing I need is for her to get involved." His gaze met mine, looking intense. "If it were up to me, you wouldn't know either."

"My wife has an uncanny knack at being present when pertinent information comes to light, and she does work with the police on an official basis quite often at home." Mitch gave me a knowing look. "That doesn't mean you interfere either, Tink. Opinions only. No action. These guys are dangerous."

"I don't know what you're talking about," I said, but we both knew that was a lie. If I thought for one moment that my friends were in danger, I would absolutely get involved.

Boomer shook his head. "I don't want Jaz involved, either. I promised her they wouldn't come to town."

"Then we handle it ourselves this time," Mitch countered, his voice filling with determination.

"Handle it how?" I asked, worry filling my gut. "You said they're watching all of us."

"A decoy," Nik suggested quietly, as if testing the word.

Boomer raised an eyebrow. "You volunteering?"

"I'm the groom. Probably not a good idea." Nik shot back, but there was a hint of a smile beneath the tension.

The idea took root, gaining momentum despite the unspoken risks attached to it.

Mitch leaned back, folding his arms. "So, we make them think we gave the drive to someone for safe keeping and then lead them on a wild goose chase."

Nik nodded. "Long enough to get through the wedding."

"And then?" I asked, needing reassurance.

"Then we lock it down," Mitch promised. "For real this time."

Boomer looked from face to face, gauging our resolve. "Alright," he said finally, a determined glint in his eyes. "Let's make it count."

Kosmos reappeared with more fries and extra napkins, giving us a questioning look.

We mumbled thanks and dug in, trying to act normal for the moment.

But my mind raced ahead wondering if Ferraro's men would bite, if they would even care about a decoy ... or if we were just delaying the inevitable fallout.

5

KALLI

A warm June breeze carried the scent of freshly cut grass and peonies as I walked the venue grounds with Jaz and Sunny, my wedding notebook clutched tightly in my hands. There were so many weddings all summer, the venue grounds remained set up. Not decorated with final touches, but the structure was ready to go. The sunlight filtered through the sprawling oak trees, casting dappled patterns across the stone pathway that led from the reception area to the church.

The setup was perfect ... so long as the mamas left things alone.

White tents lined the lawn in case of rain, with fairy lights draped across wooden pergolas, and a platform for the DJ. If the weather held, it would be magical. But despite how beautiful everything was, my nerves were frayed.

On top of that, my biological father was MIA.

He was a reformed drug dealer turned catholic priest. We had finally grown closer after he moved to Clearview, but he was away on sabbatical at the moment. I knew he would be gone for part of the summer, but he had promised to keep in touch and that he would return in time for my wedding. I hadn't heard from him in weeks.

That had me worried.

"I don't know why you're stressing," Jaz teased, looping her arm through mine. "You've helped solve murders, taken down criminals, and survived Nik's most overprotective moments. But walking down an aisle makes you anxious?"

I shot her a dry look. "Murders don't require an audience."

Sunny laughed softly, adjusting the delicate gold bracelet on her wrist. "You'll be fine, Kalli. You and Nik are meant for this." Then she paused, her expression shifting slightly.

I knew that look.

"What is it?" I asked, my stomach tensing.

Sunny's gaze flickered across the venue, like she was sensing something just out of reach. "I don't know," she murmured. "Something feels ... off today."

I knew what she meant. I kept feeling like I was being watched. Strangers were in town for the Summer Solstice Festival, so it was probably just that. Still, Sunny's psychic abilities weren't as direct as mine —she didn't read minds—but her intuition had a way of predicting trouble that always came true.

"Off how?" Jaz asked, her playful demeanor dimming just a notch.

Sunny hesitated, tucking a short blonde strand of hair behind her ear. "I can't put my finger on it. Just ... something's about to happen. I can feel it."

A chill ran down my spine despite the warmth of the sun.

I exhaled slowly. "Well, let's hope whatever it is waits until after the wedding."

We stepped inside the church, and the familiar

scent of aged wood, incense, and candle wax wrapped around me like a comforting blanket. I waved to Oswald Finch as he pushed his cart full of cleaning supplies over to one of the pews. Ozzy gave me a head nod and a smile. He was new to the diocese. Looked like a lumberjack, dark head of hair and beard to match. A bit on the shy, quiet side, but his work was spotless.

The aisle stretched ahead of us, bathed in soft light filtering through the stained-glass windows. I tried to picture it—the music playing, Nik waiting at the altar, my dress trailing behind me. But the weight in my chest didn't ease.

Then I heard it.

A muffled sob.

Frowning, I turned my head toward the altar and spotted a figure standing near one of the pews up front. Vanessa. She was hunched over slightly, her arms wrapped around herself, her back to us. A sinking feeling swept over me.

"Vanessa?" I called out gently.

She jolted as if I'd caught her stealing from the offering plate. Her hands flew to her face, wiping quickly at her cheeks before she turned to me. She pasted on a smile that didn't reach her puffy, red-rimmed eyes.

"Oh! Hey, Kalli."

Jaz and Sunny exchanged a glance, but I took a step forward.

"Are you okay?" I asked.

She let out a shaky laugh. "Wedding stress."

I frowned, feeling bad. The last thing I wanted to do was make her cry. I could tell wedding stress wasn't the whole truth. And then I saw it—dark stains on the white lace sleeve of her blouse. Jaz blinked, and Sunny's eyes grew huge.

Blood.

My pulse quickened.

"Vanessa," I said carefully, "you're bleeding."

Her eyes flickered with something—panic, maybe—before she glanced down at her sleeve like she was just now noticing it. "Oh. It's nothing, really." She quickly rolled her sleeve down. "Just a little accident."

That sounded like a lie.

"What happened?" I pressed.

She shook her head, forcing another smile. "Honestly, I don't even know. I'm just clumsy."

Before I could say more, Sunny's entire posture stiffened beside me. Her fingers twitched slightly, the way they always did when something supernatural was knocking on her subconscious.

"Where's Damon?" she asked suddenly, her voice unusually sharp.

Vanessa blinked at her. "What?"

Sunny's frown deepened. "Damon. He said he had a morning shoot for another wedding you're both working, and then he would be here to take practice shots of Kalli. Did he ever show up?"

Vanessa paled. "I—I don't know. I was running around all morning. I just assumed ..."

I glanced at Jaz, who immediately pulled out her phone. "Has anyone heard from him?"

The air in the church felt heavy, as if the walls were closing in. A creeping sense of dread curled around my spine. Then the screams started. A sharp, blood-curdling shriek cut through the air.

All three of us froze.

My body moved on instinct. I bolted out of the church, my heels clacking against the stone floor as I raced toward the parking lot, my dress rustling around my legs. I wasn't wearing my wedding dress. I was wearing a practice dress to take example photos for the big day to see what I liked best. Jaz and Sunny were right behind me, their footsteps pounding the pavement.

A small crowd had gathered near a row of parked cars, their voices a mix of confusion and fear. I pushed through the bystanders, my breath coming fast and shallow, then I stopped short when I saw him.

Damon.

His body was crammed into the open trunk of a black sedan. Vanessa's black sedan. The blood drained from my face. Damon's once-crisp white shirt was soaked in deep red blood, his body lifeless.

The world tilted slightly.

The voices around me became distant, muffled, like I was underwater.

Vanessa let out a choked sob beside me. "No. No, no, no—"

Troy stood a few feet away, his face sheet-white, his hands shaking as he pointed at the trunk. "I—I was looking for a piece of equipment I forgot. When I walked up to her car, I found him dead. Murdered. I ..." He swallowed thickly, as if unable to finish.

Sunny covered her mouth with one hand, her eyes wide with horror. Jaz whispered a prayer under her breath. My entire body was locked in place, my mind struggling to process what I was seeing.

Vanessa stumbled forward, staring at Damon's body, her breathing ragged. "Oh my God," she whispered. "No. I—this isn't—"

I turned to her, my pulse hammering. "Vanessa," I said slowly, "why is Damon in your trunk?"

She looked at me, her face stark white, her pupils blown wide with shock. "I—I don't know," she stammered. "I swear, I don't know!"

A low murmur spread through the crowd. This was bad. Really bad.

Jaz grabbed my arm, pulling me slightly aside. "Kalli," she whispered, "this doesn't look good for her."

She was right. And yet ... something wasn't adding up.

I stared at Vanessa's trembling form, at the blood still smudged on her sleeve. At the horrified look in her eyes. And in my gut, I knew—there was more to this than what we were seeing.

Sunny

The June sun blazed overhead, but a sharp chill settled deep in my bones as I knelt next to Damon's fallen camera. The smell of blood clung to the air, mingling with the scent of overheated asphalt.

My stomach churned.

My vision of the bloody trunk and blood on lace that I'd first had when the guys were in Atlantic City for Nik's bachelor party had finally come to light in the worst way. Damon's body was still crammed into the open trunk of Vanessa's car. People whispered around me, a mixture of fear and speculation thick in their voices. Vanessa was sobbing, her hands shaking, her whole body trembling as she stared at the horrible sight in front of her.

I should have comforted her.

I should have done something.

But my focus was locked on the camera.

It lay abandoned on the pavement, the lens cracked, a dark smear staining the strap. I didn't have to touch it to know it held something powerful—an imprint, an echo of whatever had happened.

I hesitated, my fingers twitching.

Mitch's voice echoed in my head, one of his many lectures over the years: *"Sunny, you can't just go touching things at crime scenes. It contaminates evidence. And one day, your visions are gonna show you something you're not ready to see."*

He was probably right.

I touched it anyway.

The world around me fractured, and suddenly, I wasn't standing in the parking lot anymore.

I was *inside* the memory.

Damon ran. His breath came in short, sharp bursts, his camera strap bouncing against his chest as he sprinted across the lot. His fingers clutched the camera tight, as if he were holding onto something crucial—something that could save him. Who was following him? It could be anyone. So many motives swam through his mind ... blackmail, betrayal, shady deals, and more. People were angry over the things he'd done. He had to get away.

He wasn't fast enough.

A figure emerged from the shadows.

"Damon, stop." *The voice was calm. Firm. Familiar, yet unclear if it was a man or a woman.*

Damon froze, his body stilling with the sharp realization of who was behind him. *"You?"* *His voice was breathless, confused.*

He never got another word out.

The first hit was sudden, a hard shove that sent him stumbling backward against a parked car. His camera slipped from his grip, hitting the pavement with a dull thud.

He gasped. *"Wait, why? I never—"*

"Oh, but you did!" *A flash of silver. The object plunged*

into his chest. Pain exploded through him, his body jerking violently. His attacker didn't hesitate. They shoved him again until he fell into the trunk. Damon's lips parted as he tried to say something, then his vision blurred, darkness creeping in at the edges.

The last thing he saw was the eyes of the person who had killed him. Eyes filled with rage. Someone he knew. Then—

Nothing.

I gasped, yanked back to reality so fast my vision swam.

Pain ghosted through my ribs where the murder weapon had struck Damon, the phantom sensation making it hard to breathe. I clenched my hands into fists, pressing my palms against the ground to keep from collapsing.

A familiar grip caught my arm, steadying me.

"Kalli," my voice came out weak.

She was already kneeling beside me, her expression tense. "What did you see?"

I sucked in a deep breath, trying to slow my pounding heart. The parking lot was spinning, the echo of Damon's final moments still burned into my mind.

"He was attacked," I managed, my throat raw. "Someone was waiting for him. He knew the person."

Kalli's face darkened, but before she could respond, the sharp, commanding voice of her fiancé sliced through the noise.

"Step back, everyone." Detective Nik Stevens strode toward us, his badge flashing in the sunlight.

Behind him, Mitch and Boomer flanked either side, their expressions grim. The moment they arrived, the energy in the parking lot shifted. The mur-

murs quieted. The bystanders instinctively moved back, sensing the weight of authority.

Mitch's sharp gaze flickered to me, then to the camera I'd dropped beside me.

His jaw clenched. "Sunny," he said tightly. "Tell me you *didn't* just touch evidence."

I swallowed. "I—I couldn't help it."

Nik let out a sharp breath, his gaze moving to the open trunk, to Damon's body. His face was unreadable, but I saw the subtle tightening of his shoulders —the only sign that he was affected.

"She found the body?" Nik asked, jerking his head in Vanessa's direction.

Troy took a step forward, still looking shaken. "I did. I thought I left some equipment behind and—I popped the trunk, and ..." He trailed off, running a hand through his hair.

Boomer muttered a curse, shaking his head.

Mitch crouched beside the trunk, his usual relaxed demeanor replaced with something much colder. "Cause of death looks like a stab wound to the chest," he observed, his voice clinical. He glanced at Nik. "Time of death estimate?"

Nik exhaled. "Coroner will confirm, but given the lividity, I'd say after midnight, in the early hours of the morning."

Vanessa let out a strangled sob. "I didn't do this," she blurted, her voice cracking. "I swear, I didn't—"

Boomer held up a hand. "Vanessa, I need you to calm down."

Her breathing turned erratic. "My car was locked! I —I don't know how he got in there."

Mitch and Boomer exchanged a look.

"She's the only one with access to the vehicle," Mitch pointed out, his voice unreadable.

"That's not true." Vanessa's voice rose in panic. "Troy drove it last night. He had the spare key."

Boomer's face remained neutral, but I knew the unspoken decision had already been made. The body was in *her* car. She had blood on her sleeve.

Vanessa was the prime suspect.

Nik sighed, rubbing a hand down his face. "We'll have to take you in for questioning."

Vanessa paled. "No, please. This is insane. I didn't like Damon, but I would never hurt anyone." She turned to Kalli and me, her eyes pleading. "You *know* me."

I watched her closely. The tremble in her hands. The raw, unfiltered terror in her eyes. This wasn't guilt. It was shock. Real shock. Kalli and I locked eyes for a brief second, and I knew she felt it too.

This didn't add up.

Mitch stepped forward, his voice softer than Nik's. "Vanessa, come with us. We'll talk at the station."

Her shoulders slumped, her breath hitching as she nodded weakly. She didn't fight as Nik led her toward the squad car.

The crowd started dispersing, but an unease lingered in the air.

Kalli crossed her arms. "This doesn't feel right."

I shook my head. "Because it isn't."

I thought of my vision—the precision of the attack, the control, the rage. It was conflicting. Precision and control indicated someone who wanted Damon silenced, but rage indicated it was personal. A crime of passion. Either way, the person who did it was still out there ...

And we had no idea if they were finished.

6

KALLI

The cold air hit my skin as we stepped into the *Clearview Police Department*, a stark contrast to the warmth of the coffee shop we'd left behind. We brought sustenance for the uncomfortable conversations ahead. The fluorescent lights overhead buzzed faintly, casting a harsh glow over the dull gray walls and scuffed linoleum floor. The entire building smelled like stale coffee and cheap disinfectant.

Nik, Boomer, and Mitch led the way, their postures rigid, their expressions unreadable. Sunny, Jaz, and I trailed behind them, the quiet thud of our footsteps echoing down the hall. Tension coiled in my stomach. This wasn't just some casual questioning—this was about our wedding photographer.

About murder.

Nik pushed open the interrogation room door, revealing Troy sitting at the metal table.

Troy looked worse than I expected—his dark eyes were rimmed with exhaustion, his fingers strumming the tabletop, and his knee bouncing anxiously beneath it. His dark red hair was disheveled, and his jaw was tight, like he was clenching his teeth to keep himself together. He swallowed hard when he saw us enter, his gaze sweeping to Nik before dropping to his lap.

Nik didn't waste time. He pulled out a chair across from Troy, the metal scraping against the tile as he sat down. Boomer and Mitch stood behind him, arms crossed.

"Alright, Troy," Nik started, his voice steady but firm. "Walk me through this again. You borrowed Vanessa's car the day before the murder. Why?"

Troy rubbed the back of his neck. "My car broke down," he said. His voice was hoarse, like he hadn't slept or had been talking in circles for too long. "I didn't want Damon to be mad at me for not getting the photography equipment to the church on time, so I asked Vanessa if I could use her car."

"Did she hesitate?" Boomer asked, tilting his head.

Troy shook his head quickly. "No, she was cool about it. She just told me to leave it at the church when I was done. So, I took the equipment to *Holy Trinity*, unloaded it, and then walked home."

Boomer leaned in slightly. "Walked home from the church?"

"Yeah," Troy said, nodding. "I live a few blocks away. It's not that far. Vanessa does, too."

Mitch scribbled something in his notebook. "And you were home all night?"

"Yes," Troy said immediately.

I folded my arms. "No calls? No messages? No one who can confirm that?"

His throat bobbed as he swallowed. "No," he admitted. "I was alone."

A heavy silence filled the room.

Nik's gaze stayed on Troy. "And the next morning?"

Troy ran a hand down his face. "I woke up and realized I left a piece of equipment in the car. Stupid mistake. I didn't want Damon to flip out, so I went to the venue early morning to grab it. I used the spare key Vanessa had given me to unlock the car." He hesitated, his fingers curling into fists. "And that's when I found him."

The words hung in the air like a thick fog.

Jaz shifted beside me, her sharp gaze narrowing. "You just opened the trunk and there he was?"

"Yeah," Troy said, his voice cracking. "I mean, I wasn't expecting it. I thought maybe I left the equipment in the backseat, but when I didn't see it, I figured I'd check the trunk. And—and he was just ... there." His hands trembled slightly as he rubbed them together. "I panicked. I didn't even process it at first. Just ... I don't know. It didn't feel real."

A chill ran down my spine.

Nik leaned forward, his fingers interlocked. "Did you touch anything?"

Troy shook his head furiously. "No! I swear! I—I just backed away and called the police." He let out a humorless laugh, one that sounded more like a choked breath. "What else was I supposed to do?"

I studied him carefully, searching for any flicker of dishonesty in his expression. He looked genuinely shaken, but was he telling the whole truth?

Nik nodded slowly, making a note as Troy was taken from the room, and then glanced at Mitch. "Alright. Let's bring in Vanessa."

A few minutes later, Vanessa entered the room.

She was composed, but there was something in her eyes—something raw, like she'd been barely holding it together. Her usually neat, professional attire was slightly wrinkled, and she clutched her hands tightly in her lap.

Nik sat across from her. "Vanessa, you lent your car to Troy the day before the murder. And you didn't use it at all that night?"

She shook her head. "No. I was home all night."

Boomer tapped his pen against his notepad. "And you planned to pick it up the next morning?"

"Yes," she said. "Troy was finished with it, and I didn't need it the night before. I was going to the venue early anyway, so I figured I'd get it then."

"You went to *Holy Trinity* early?" I asked.

Vanessa hesitated and then nodded. "Yeah. I wanted some time alone before my day began. It's been overwhelming lately."

Sunny tilted her head. "Why?"

Vanessa exhaled, her fingers tightening. "Personal reasons. Wedding stress."

"Is that when you cut yourself?" I looked at her sleeve.

"I didn't even notice I was bleeding until you did. I told you I am clumsy." Her voice dropped slightly. "I just needed a moment to breathe."

Nik frowned. "We'll need to test that for DNA."

"Of course." She nodded.

Mitch studied her. "What time did you get there?"

"Around seven," she said.

"Did you check your car when you arrived?"

Vanessa frowned slightly. "No. I wasn't leaving yet, so I didn't bother."

Boomer's expression remained neutral, but I could see the gears turning in his head. "Was the car locked?"

"Yes," Vanessa said immediately, and then frowned. "Or at least I assume so. I told Troy to lock it when he was done."

"And Troy got in with the spare key you gave him," Jaz added.

Vanessa nodded, rubbing her temples. "Yes. I gave it to him the day before."

Nik sat back, his fingers tapping against the table. "Which means, he might have forgotten to lock it the night before. Someone else could have accessed the car after he left and then locked it."

Vanessa's eyes widened slightly. "I—I guess so. But I swear I had no idea Damon was in there. I didn't understand what was happening until we heard screams and ran outside to see Troy standing by the open trunk with Damon lying lifeless inside."

Now that they had both been questioned, Nik had Troy brought back into the room and recounted Vanessa's version of the events.

Troy let out a bitter laugh. "She didn't understand what was happening? Try being me." His eyes met hers. "I nearly lost my breakfast, and I'm pretty sure I locked your car the night before."

A heavy silence settled among us.

Nik closed his notebook with a quiet snap. "Alright. We'll need to verify your alibis and check for any additional security footage."

Vanessa bit her lip, her voice barely above a whisper. "You don't think I had anything to do with this ... do you?"

Nik didn't answer right away. "We're just covering all possibilities."

Vanessa looked down, her hands gripping each other tightly.

I couldn't shake the unease settling in my gut. If neither Vanessa nor Troy had used the car after midnight, then that meant someone else had access to it.

Someone who had a key or knew how to pick a lock or knew the car was unlocked.

And that someone had murdered Damon and shoved his body in the trunk.

"All right, Troy, you are free to go but don't leave town," Nik said, turning to Vanessa. "We'll have to hold you a little longer until we test the blood on your shirt." He scanned the room. "The rest of you stay. We need to put our heads together."

Sunny

The air in the *Clearview Police Department* felt heavier now, thick with tension and the sharp scent of coffee gone cold and stale. The overhead fluorescent lights still buzzed faintly, casting even harsher white light over the gray walls and scuffed floors now.

Everyone had taken five minutes and reconvened in the conference room. The men were refilling their coffee cups and comparing notes. Kalli sat stiffly in a chair, her arms wrapped around herself like she was holding everything in, her green eyes unfocused. She was trying to be strong, but I could feel the weight pressing down on her.

Jaz knelt in front of her, with her hands covering Kalli's. "Breathe, okay?" she murmured. "This is a lot. I know that, but we've got you. We'll get through this."

Kalli let out a shaky breath, her lips pressed into a thin line. "I keep thinking about how this was supposed to be one of the happiest times of my life," she admitted, her voice tight. "And now the place I picked to get married in is a crime scene. Every time I close my eyes, I see Damon in that trunk." She swallowed. "This isn't how it was supposed to be."

Jaz squeezed her hands. "I know, but this doesn't define your wedding, Kalli. You and Nik—what you have is real. This ... this is just a storm you have to get through."

I wanted to say something reassuring too, but my thoughts were elsewhere. The tingling sensation from my earlier vision still lingered in my fingertips, an eerie aftershock of what I'd seen when I touched Damon's camera.

Blackmail, betrayal, and shady deals.

The vision was fragmented—like looking through a foggy mirror—but the emotions were crystal clear. Fear. Anger. Desperation. I didn't see Damon actually threatening someone, but the feelings of being blackmailed had been there, and now he was dead. That wasn't a coincidence. He knew his killer, and they had been filled with rage. I wasn't sure if the killer was the same person Damon was blackmailing or someone blackmailing him, but I *was* sure he had made his fair share of enemies.

I pulled out my tarot deck from my bag, the familiar weight of the cards grounding me. My fingers moved through them instinctively, shuffling with practiced ease. Then I drew a card. The Tower ... again. My stomach clenched.

Chaos. Upheaval. A complete destruction of the current order.

The Tower didn't warn of small problems—it foretold events that shattered foundations. Whatever was happening here, whatever had gotten Damon killed, wasn't finished yet. Before I could say anything, the door swung open, and two people entered the room.

Nik, Boomer, and Mitch looked at the door then took their seats at the conference table.

Captain Quincy Crenshaw's presence filled the space immediately. He was a tall, broad-shouldered man in his fifties, his graying hair cropped close, his steel gray eyes scanning the room with authority. He moved with a quiet confidence that demanded respect.

Behind him, Mayor Flynn Zimmerman followed, her sophisticated face set in a scowl. The woman had an ever-present air of impatience, and today was no different. Her tailored navy suit that matched her eyes was immaculate, her cropped silver hair gleaming under the fluorescent lights.

Crenshaw's gaze landed on Nik first. "Detective Stevens," he said, his voice steady. "Tell me you have something. The mayor wants an update on the murder investigation with the summer season in full swing." He might be engaged to Nik's ma, but when it came to the job, he was all business.

Nik, ever composed, leaned back against the desk, his arms crossed. "We're still working through the details, Captain," he replied. "We've questioned Troy and Vanessa. Their stories align, but their alibis aren't solid. There's blood on Vanessa's shirt we'll test as well, but she says it's not Damon's. Claims it's her own. Either way, she still could have killed him and cut herself in the process. She did have a scrape on her arm."

Zimmerman let out an exaggerated huff. "That's not good enough. The press is already picking up whispers of this, and we can't afford a scandal right now. This is supposed to be a place of worship, baptisms, and holy unions, not a crime scene. Not a good look for our town, especially during the start of the summer season."

Jaz narrowed her eyes at her. "With all due respect, Ms. Mayor, a man is dead. I think that's a little more important than your PR problem."

Zimmerman's face turned red, but Crenshaw held up a hand, cutting her off. "What about other leads?"

Boomer flipped through his notepad. "We're considering multiple angles. Right now, Vanessa is our prime suspect since the car belonged to her and her bloody sleeve. And Troy is a person of interest, but we're expanding our suspect pool."

Mitch crossed his arms. "We need to look into Barry Franklin, the DJ. He was at the venue the night before and in the early morning with his assistant, Josh. He had access, and he made it clear he thought Damon was a diva."

"Not to mention Lila Cross," Nik added. "Damon's ex-wife. Their divorce wasn't exactly amicable, and she didn't seem too broken up about his death when we spoke to her before coming here."

Crenshaw arched a brow. "You think she could've done it?"

"She had motive," Nik said. "Damon wasn't just her ex—he was still in her life in ways she didn't want him to be. She comes from money. He was suing her for more alimony, and she was *livid* about it."

"She told me she had no reason to want him dead," I mused, tilting my head. "But her aura said otherwise. She's hiding something."

Zimmerman scoffed. "Aura? Really? This is a murder investigation, not a séance. All due respect, but this isn't your town. Your husband's either."

I gave her my best unimpressed stare. "And yet, I'm usually right about these things. Detective Stevens helped Divinity's police department a while back. My husband is only trying to return the favor unofficially."

"I say we can use all the help we can get." Crenshaw, unlike Zimmerman, actually listened. "Murder weapon?"

"He was stabbed, but no weapon was found at the scene," Mitch said.

"What about other staff at the venue?" the captain asked. "Any leads there?"

Nik nodded. "We're looking into Angela Reynolds, the seamstress. She was around the venue a lot and was seen arguing with Damon earlier that week. And then there's Marcus Eldridge—the real estate developer. He's handling the parish center renovation, so he's always around."

Boomer exhaled sharply. "Eldridge had a real reason to want Damon gone. Damon was telling people he had dirt on Eldridge. Who knows if it was true or not, but rumors are still damaging."

Crenshaw's jaw tightened. "So, Damon was stirring up trouble on multiple fronts. Somehow that doesn't surprise me."

"Seems that way," Nik agreed.

I took a deep breath, looking at the others. "Damon betrayed someone and was blackmailing at least one person, maybe more."

The room fell silent.

Nik's eyes snapped to mine. "What?"

"I saw it," I admitted. "When I touched Damon's camera, I had a vision of his death. I didn't see the person, but Damon was worried about who was chasing him, and he definitely recognized his killer. I don't know if it was the same person he was blackmailing or not, but it's a start." I looked at Crenshaw. "Whoever he was blackmailing—they're the one we need to find first."

Crenshaw nodded, a muscle in his jaw tightening. "This just keeps getting messier."

Zimmerman grumbled something under her breath, clearly unimpressed, but I didn't care what she thought. I was used to dealing with non-believers. Nik and Kalli didn't want an unsolved murder hovering over their wedding, and I had visions that could help.

So that's what I intended to keep doing, whether the mayor liked it or not.

7

KALLI

There's something dangerous about mixing family, feta, and feelings. Try telling that to a Greek mama. The backyard at my parents' house looked like a Mediterranean wedding catalog had exploded. They were going all out, trying to impress Sunny's family.

The white gazebo was trimmed in blue and gold streamers, and twinkle lights draped from every tree and post, even though it was brunch and the sun was blinding. A white marble fountain burbled beside the patio, where Poseidon stood mid-splash, riding a dolphin like he was late to a party.

Statues of Greek gods flanked the edges of the yard like stone chaperones. Pop had installed them along with Poseidon in the fountain recently after he took Ma on an anniversary trip to Athens, and they'd become unofficial family members. Dionysus stood beside the grill, and Ma had once tied a baby bib around Hermes during my cousin's baptism luncheon.

The smell of oregano, garlic, lemon, grilled meats, and powdered sugar was so thick in the air it made my eyes water. Platters lined the table under the gazebo: skewers of souvlaki, pastitsio, dolmades, flaky spanakopita, and a literal mountain of baklava. There were bowls of olives and tubs of tzatziki, every carb known to man, and enough goat cheese to feed an actual goat.

Nik sat beside me, looking amused. Boomer and Jaz were across from us, trying to strategize how to politely decline their third serving of lamb without invoking a mama's wrath. Sunny and Mitch lounged near the fountain under a shaded pergola with the Tasty Trio who were already passing around mimosas and planning a spa day.

All the pets played with the children in the yard.

The breeze carried the tinkling of laughter and the occasional clang of metal from the outdoor kitchen, where my pop, papou, brother Jasper, and cousins were arguing about how long to grill the octopus. I should've waited until everyone had plates in hand and mouths full of food before dropping my news, but of course, I didn't.

"I've been thinking about the wedding," I said. Just five words. A soft, casual sentence. You would think I'd set off a bomb.

Everything stopped.

Everyone stared.

Like a power outage in a restaurant—voices silenced, forks froze mid-air, and even the Poseidon fountain sputtered at the worst possible moment.

Ma slowly lowered her frappé, her mouth falling open. Aunt Tasoula dropped her fork with an audible *clink* onto her plate of pastitsio. Chloe, never one to be outdone, let out a faint gasp and immediately grabbed the lace mourning veil she kept in her handbag like other women carried ibuprofen.

I braced myself.

"I've been thinking," I said again, quieter this time.

"With everything that's been going on ... with Damon's murder, the investigation, the stress ... maybe it's not the right time to get married." Nik's family would have to change their tickets, and the venders might not be happy about cancelled orders, but I had to put myself and my mental health first.

The Greek mamas reacted as if I'd told them I was becoming a nun and moving to Siberia.

Aunt Tasoula slapped both hands on the table. "*Panagia mou!* The engagement cursed! I told you we should burn the evil eye during lunar eclipse! Now the gods angry."

Ma's eyes filled with tears instantly. "You breaking you yiayia's heart! She crochet you bridal hand-kerchief!"

Chloe moaned dramatically, draping the veil over her head. "*The omens! The omens!* You wore blue nail polish in engagement photos! That was warning!"

Boomer leaned toward Nik and whispered, but I heard him, "Should I shield you, buddy? You might be the sacrificial offering."

Nik didn't even blink. "No way am I getting between Kalli and the mamas. And I have to say I'm not very happy with the idea of canceling the wedding, either." He frowned. "She should have talked to me first."

Oh, my Zeus. What had I done?

Across the table, the Tasty Trio sat slack-jawed in their Sunday dresses, pantsuits, and aprons.

"You're *postponing* the wedding?" Fiona squeaked, like she couldn't fathom the words.

"No, she said *maybe*," Granny Gert clarified, already spiraling. "Oh, dear. This is like that time my cousin called off her wedding and the whole family broke out in shingles. I'll have to bake some cookies to protect us from that."

"I made a custom playlist!" Fiona wailed. "Do you know how hard it is to mix Beyoncé with traditional bouzouki? I had a theme. It was called *Modern Mythology*!"

"And I brought my dancing shoes," Great Grandma Tootsie said. "Boys oh day, what if I don't get a chance to wear them again. I am a century, after all."

"I'm not saying I *don't* want to marry Nik," I said quickly, raising my hands like I was trying to calm a herd of runaway goats. "I do. I love him. I just—I need to breathe. Every day lately has been stress and crime scenes and cake tastings and—" My voice cracked. "And I found a fingerprint on the ring bearer's pillow next to a tray of *koufeta*." I blinked back tears. "I can't get the stain out."

Nik finally took my hand under the table and gave it a gentle squeeze. "If you want to postpone, you know I'll support you. You come first, Ballas. Not the wedding. Not the food. Not even the koufeta." *I've got you, babe.*

I smiled my appreciation and squeezed his hand back.

Ma clutched her chest like Nik had just proposed to me all over again. "He so perfect," she whispered. "Just like my Jasper. He no find nice Greek girl either." Emily, the social media influencer he'd been dating, had decided he wasn't famous enough for her anymore and had moved on.

"Tragic," Chloe sniffled. "My perfect Greek boy, and still she cancel. What wrong with her?"

"There's nothing wrong with me, and I'm not *cancelling*," I said. "Just ... maybe pushing it back. Or scaling it down. Or eloping quietly and reemerging at the reception in disguise."

The Tasty Trio gasped.

The mamas made the sign of the cross.

I groaned, mentally slapping my forehead.

Sunny joined our table, setting down her mimosa. Her gold bangles chimed softly. "Kalli, honey, listen. A wedding should be a celebration of love, not a battle. You're allowed to take a moment, but make sure it's about healing, not fear."

Mitch nodded beside her, ever the steady detective. "We've seen a lot of people crash under pressure. You two aren't them. But that doesn't mean you don't get to slow down."

"Life lesson #10," Great Grandma Tootsie said, adjusting her scarf. "A Pinterest board is not a plan for emotional health."

"Life lesson #22," Granny Gert added, smoothing down her apron. "Nothing good comes from making decisions while overwhelmed and overfed."

"Don't forget life lesson #5," Fiona chimed in, patting her chic hairdo. "Always test your spray tan on your *back* before committing to a strapless dress." She winked.

A beat passed. Then Chloe lifted the veil just enough to glare at them. "This no time for self-tanning advice. There no honeymoon if there no wedding."

Nik leaned toward me again, holding my hand. "Whatever you decide, I'm there." *Whether it's a wedding in a couple weeks or a taco truck elopement in Mexico in three months. You're it for me. The details don't matter.*

My throat tightened. Darn him! He really was perfect. "I just want to feel like this is our wedding again," I said quietly. "Not just some party planned by our mamas that we're surviving while solving murders in our free time."

"Then let's take it back," he said. "On our terms."

Ma sniffled and handed me a buttered roll. "Fine. But promise me you still wear my dress. It blessed with holy water and sequins."

"And still have baklava tower," Aunt Tasoula added solemnly. "That pastry architect no cheap but so worth it."

"Let's toast," Jaz said brightly, raising her glass. "In honor of emotional clarity and regaining sanity."

"*And love!*" Chloe sobbed.

We all raised a glass—coffee, mimosa, or orange juice—and clinked in unison.

The mourning veil stayed on the table.

Poseidon resumed burbling.

And for the first time in days, I felt the knot in my chest loosen.

I wasn't running away from my wedding. I was finding my way back to it. Back to what I wanted, the way I wanted it, on my terms.

Sunny

We'd all planned on staying in Clearview until the wedding, so nothing changed on our end. We were here to support Kalli and Nik, but also help with the investigation. Something about Damon's murder clung to all of us like fog that hadn't burned off. I knew it in my bones—this wasn't just a one-and-done mystery. This case had layers.

And right now, the layer in front of me was named *Lila Cross.*

I spotted her just past the café, making her way down Main Street with the forced elegance of a woman trying very hard not to look rushed—or watched. Her white linen pantsuit was pressed to perfection, her scarf knotted just so, and her oversized sunglasses covered half her face. A designer bag swung against her hip, and her sandals clicked on the pavement like punctuation.

She was trying to look effortless, but her aura was pulsing with nerves.

We were supposed to be heading to the bakery. Zoe walked beside me, pushing baby Alannah in her stroller, while Jo herded her twins—Collin and Jeremiah—with the tired precision of a mother who had surrendered to the madness of twin boys and made peace with it. Tina skipped beside me in her pink polka-dot dress, claiming boys were annoying, and River was in my arms, heavy and warm, giggling into my shoulder.

But when I saw Lila, something shifted. That sixth sense of mine—my compass when logic fails—flickered to life.

"Sunny," Jo called gently. "You're drifting off the path."

"I know," I said under my breath, keeping my eyes on Lila.

She paused outside one of the boutiques and leaned closer to the window, pretending to study a trinket displayed under glass. But I could tell—she was watching her reflection. Watching *us*.

I slowed, pretending to scroll through my phone.

Lila pivoted slightly, clearly trying to stay casual. That's when a door creaked open across the street.

"Lila Cross?" a voice called out—shrill, unmistakable, and Greek.

We all turned as Despina Lambros poked her perfectly coiffed head out of the side door of her *Lambros Yarn-and-Card Shop*. She wore her usual ensemble: a Mediterranean blue cardigan and a strand of pearls big enough to anchor a boat. Ophelia had introduced her to me at Aphrodite's during the welcome reception, and Kalli had filled me in on the rest.

Despina was famous for two things: running the Thursday night Biriba Club after hours in her shop and knowing *everybody's* business before they did.

"Lila Cross," she called again, louder now, to no one in particular but very much on purpose. "I saw you outside *Damon's Dreams Studio* just last week. You were yelling about money. Don't act like I hallucinate; I had my readers on and everything."

Lila flinched. "Despina, you must be mistaken," she snapped, turning on her heel. "I haven't seen Damon in *months*."

Despina snorted, unbothered. "Honey, I don't miss things. You were waving that crocodile handbag around like you were possessed by Hades. I nearly called Father Papadopoulos to perform an exorcism!"

Lila let out a dramatic huff and took off down the sidewalk.

Jo glanced at Zoe.

Zoe arched a brow at me.

"I'm following her," I muttered. We were on a main street, during daylight, with several people milling about. It was safe enough not to let this opportunity slip by.

Neither of them said a word. Zoe adjusted her hands on Alannah's stroller, and Jo tightened her grip on the twins, ready to follow me anywhere. No questions asked. That's what best friends do.

I situated River on my hip and picked up the pace.

Jo fell in behind with her boys, who were now chattering and pointing at a chalk mural someone had drawn near the lampposts in between poking each other. Tina kept up with ease, skipping along beside me and humming to herself like none of this was even a little bit strange.

Just as I rounded the corner, River let out a bubbling laugh that made his whole belly shake.

"What's funny, little man?" I asked, brushing a kiss against his forehead.

"He's just goofy, Mama," Tina said matter-of-factly. "Like Uncle Sean."

I chuckled. "You're not wrong."

But River kept giggling, wiggling in my arms until he pointed forward. Not at Lila. Not at her scarf. At her *purse.*

Lila stopped at a flower cart to study the bouquets. I quickened my pace and passed her, my shoulder skimming hers—and my fingers, without thinking, brushed the side of her bag. The moment I touched it, I knew.

A jolt of cold, spiraling emotion shot through me—anxiety like a flood, desperation that tasted metallic, fear that pressed against my ribs like a hand clamping down. My heart stuttered. My skin tingled.

I blinked, breaking the spell.

Damon had threatened her.

She was scared—genuinely scared. Not just of possible consequences for what she had done. But for what she was about to do.

Lila ducked into *Nelson's Jewelers* without so much as a glance back at us, none the wiser of the vision I'd just had.

I stopped outside the shop, my heart thudding. Inside, light bounced off glass cases filled with engagement rings, antique brooches, and those ridiculously expensive bracelets they never actually sell.

Zoe rolled up beside me with the stroller, lowering her sunglasses as she stared through the window. "Okay, is she ... buying something?"

Jo came up behind us with the twins in tow, shaking her head. "Didn't Nik say she filed for bankruptcy a few weeks ago? Like, crying-at-city-hall paperwork filed?"

I nodded absently, as I watched Lila gesture toward the clerk with a quick, clipped motion. "He also said even though she comes from old family money, Lila told Kalli she was 'simplifying her life.'"

Jo snorted. "Yet she's picking out diamonds? That doesn't make sense."

Zoe leaned on the stroller handle. "Maybe she's not buying anything."

We all watched as Lila passed a small envelope across the counter. Nelson wasn't in today. The clerk opened it, squinted, and then reached under the counter for a loupe.

"She's pawning something," Jo confirmed, her eyes narrowing. "Trying to get fast cash."

Tina tugged on my arm again, her voice soft. "Mama? Why are we peeking through windows like Daddy?"

I looked down at her sweet, curious face. "We're just window shopping, honey."

"But we already have windows." Tina frowned. "Are you goofy like River?"

I laughed at my observant daughter, so like her father. "Probably so, my darling."

River had gone quiet again, sucking on his thumb and resting his cheek against my shoulder. I could still feel the leftover current from that purse—like a storm cloud trapped in leather.

Lila emerged from the store moments later, her face pinched and unsmiling as she slid her sunglasses back in place. She clutched the envelope tightly, like whatever was inside had the power to solve all her problems ...

Or bury them.

She didn't see us as she turned in the opposite direction. Or if she *did* see us, she pretended not to.

"She's not just nervous," I said under my breath. "She's *in trouble*. And not just because she argued with Damon."

Jo folded her arms. "I say we bring it to Mitch. Let him, Nik, and Boomer poke around. Maybe they missed something the first time."

Zoe looked at me. "What do you think?"

I watched Lila's retreating figure disappear into the curve of Main Street, the hem of her scarf fluttering like a white flag.

"I think," I said slowly, "Lila Cross is either running out of time ..." I paused, resting my cheek gently against River's soft curls, "... or options."

Or maybe both.

8

KALLI

The air in Marcus Eldridge's office smelled like expensive cologne and furniture polish, a sharp contrast to the faint floral breeze drifting in through the windows. Everything here was calculated—glass shelves filled with sleek architectural models, a wall-mounted TV silently looping images of Clearview's waterfront, and not a speck of dust in sight. It didn't feel like an office.

It felt like a showroom.

Jaz stood beside me, her arms crossed, her gaze cool as ice, fiercely protective. She hadn't sat down, and she wasn't planning to. I knew that stance—she was two seconds from dismantling this man with her words.

Marcus Eldridge stood behind his desk, leaning slightly against the edge as if to appear casual, but nothing about him was relaxed. His hands moved constantly—tapping, fidgeting, checking his phone every thirty seconds like he was waiting for something.

Or someone.

"So," Jaz said finally, breaking the silence, her voice edged with challenge. "Let me get this straight. You got into a screaming match with Damon before he died, and now you're super invested in this wedding continuing? Why?"

Marcus's jaw ticked. "The parish center remodel is important to my business, and the wedding reception is the first event taking place there. That's all."

I stepped forward, folding my hands in front of me. "Your business? You mean real estate?"

He nodded curtly. "Yes. The church, the surrounding properties, the revitalization of downtown—this wedding brings eyes. Media. Money. I've put a lot of effort into elevating this town's image. A high-profile wedding helps."

"High profile?" I raised a brow at him.

"The Ballas and Pagonis families make up half this town. Your families carry a lot of weight in this community, so I'd say that makes your wedding important," he said.

I laughed a bit hysterically. Eloping really was looking better and better.

Jaz let out a short, humorless laugh. "So ... murder at the parish center is good PR now?"

Marcus's eyes narrowed. "I'm not saying the murder helps, but scrapping the event entirely? That sends a message that Clearview isn't stable. That it's not the kind of town worth investing in." He paused. "I've worked too hard to let one tragedy ruin it."

Event? This wasn't an event ... this was my life. I sighed, studying him. His voice was steady, but his fingers still lingered near the edge of his phone.

"You said you and Damon had a disagreement. Over what exactly? I asked.

He lifted his chin a little too quickly. "Marketing ideas. I saw a broader potential than Damon. Father Papadopoulos and the entire diocese were on the fence about expanding events held at the new and improved center. But after almost having to shut down because of the snake infestation drama, they were close to agreeing. I needed Damon's help to convince them, but just to spite me, Damon sided with them in keeping the church reserved for cultural events only—strictly Greek Orthodox weddings and festivals."

"Why did Damon's opinion matter?" I asked.

"Damon was involved in far more than just photography. He had pull. Connections. We could've done so much more with the space."

Jaz arched a brow. "So, he refused to work with you, and you killed him?"

Marcus's mouth flattened. "It wasn't that dramatic."

"Multiple witnesses say otherwise," Jaz muttered. "You were screaming at him on the church steps the day before he died."

Marcus straightened. "Because he was being shortsighted. Emotional. I don't have anything to hide, and I certainly don't have to answer to you two."

Really? You certainly look guilty, I thought, but I didn't say it. Instead, I watched his hands. The way he kept curling and uncurling his fingers. His shoulders were too stiff. The tension in his jaw hadn't eased once since we arrived. I trusted my gut.

And right now, my gut was screaming that he wasn't telling the whole truth.

"It doesn't matter if you talk to us or not." Jaz took a step back. "The truth always comes out in the end."

Marcus reached for his phone the second we turned.

As we moved toward the door, something on the bookshelf caught my eye—a glossy silver frame half-hidden behind an abstract sculpture. I paused, taking a closer look. It was a photo of Marcus and Damon, standing shoulder to shoulder at what looked like a local charity event. The banner in the background read *Clearview Community Rising Gala*.

They were both smiling—genuinely smiling—and shaking hands.

"They weren't always enemies," Jaz murmured, stepping up beside me. "So, what happened?"

I stared at the photo for a moment. There was no tension there. No resentment. They looked like partners. Allies.

"We need to find out," I said quietly.

We exited into the bright light of day, blinking against the sun. The contrast between the sterile chill of Marcus's office and the warmth outside felt jarring. The breeze carried the scent of blooming peonies from the florist down the street and the clinking of silverware from the café patio where tourists sipped iced coffee under umbrellas.

"Hey, Kalli!"

We turned to see Wendy hurrying across the street with a giant bouquet of white garden roses, eucalyptus, and blue delphinium. The stems were wrapped in white satin and trailing ribbons in soft gold.

She grinned at me as she crossed the sidewalk. "On my way to the Thompson wedding, but I need your final decision for your own bouquet, stat. I know you're paused or whatever, but if you wait too long, the June florals are gonna bolt right out of season."

I smiled weakly. "I'll call you tomorrow."

"You said that yesterday."

"I mean it this time."

She gave me a look that said *I've worked with too many brides to believe that,* and then she disappeared into the church, the scent of the bouquet lingering behind her.

Jaz raised a brow. "Planning a wedding and solving a murder. Want to add a marathon to your to-do list while you're at it?"

I didn't respond. I was too focused on what—or who—I saw halfway down the block.

Troy.

He was hunched near the entrance to Damon's studio, crouched at the lock with what looked like a key in one hand and his phone in the other. His eyes darted up when he heard us approaching. He jumped to his feet like a kid caught sneaking cookies.

"Oh—hey," he said, a little too brightly. "Didn't see you there."

"What are you doing?" Jaz asked, her tone already sharp.

"Just ... checking on the studio." He scratched the back of his neck. "Lila and I talked. She's letting me handle Damon's outstanding contracts—weddings, portraits, business shoots. It's what Damon would've wanted. He was going to make me a partner before ... before everything."

"A partner?" I echoed. Last I knew Damon was mad at him for making more than one careless mistake.

He nodded quickly. "Yeah. He said it a few times. Nothing official, but it was in the works. I've been shadowing him for a year. I know how he ran things. Clients have been reaching out. They want someone they trust, and that's me."

I stepped closer, my instinct pulling me in. "You're buying the business?"

"Trying to," he said. "Technically, Lila owns it now. Damon never changed his will, so it went to her and the kids, but she doesn't want it. She said if I could keep it going, she'd sell."

Something about the way he said it felt ... slippery.

I pretended to stumble and reached out to grab onto his arm, pushing thoughts of germs aside for the sake of justice.

"Whoa, easy there," he said, helping me up but I could tell he was in his head, and his thoughts confirmed it. *I still can't believe Damon was going to fire me. Said I wasn't focused just because the last three clients complained about missed deadlines and over-edited photos. What did he expect with overworking and underpaying me? I begged him for another chance. Told him I'd fix everything. I have plans. I need this. If Lila thinks it was his wish, she'll sell it to me for cheap.*

"Thanks," I replied and let go of his arm slowly, my heart sinking. "Troy," I said carefully, "are you sure Damon really wanted you to take over? Not just ... trying to let you down easy?"

He blinked. "Of course, I'm sure."

Jaz narrowed her eyes. "It's convenient, isn't it? He dies before any paperwork's signed, and suddenly you're the heir to his business dreams."

His smile faltered. "Look, I'm just trying to keep things running. People need photos, including you." He looked at me, adding with a shrug, "Life goes on."

"For some," Jaz muttered.

We let him walk away without another word. He disappeared into the crowd, his lie still ringing in my ears.

Damon had planned to end Troy's contract. He didn't trust him. He *wasn't* handing over the business. I had so many questions. Why was Troy pretending? How far would he go to make that story true?

We were getting closer to the truth. I could feel it. But the closer we got, the more I realized—this wasn't just about a murder. It was about everything Damon left behind ...

And who was willing to lie, steal, or kill to claim it.

Sunny

The *Clearview Hotel* lobby was cozy. Kalli said the manager, Gary Bolin, was a friend of hers and had remodeled it when he had taken it over. It was cozy, but not fancy. Not anything like Domonic Ferraro was used to, which made it neutral territory, quiet, and out of sight from Ferraro's men.

That made it safe enough—for now.

River sat on Mitch's lap at the small sitting area near the window, humming as he squeezed his stuffed hound dog, while Tina colored at the coffee table with the seriousness of a courtroom sketch artist. She was deep into her "draw Kalli's wedding dress" phase and currently shading something that looked like a veil covered in jellybeans.

Boomer leaned against a support pillar near the fireplace, his arms crossed and eyes sharp. Nik sat across from me, flipping through the latest case file from the murder scene. There was more paperwork than progress, and we all felt it. Kalli knew about Ferraro and his henchmen from the bachelor party, but she didn't know they had been spotted in Clearview.

Nik was determined to keep it that way.

"They've been tailing me again," Boomer said finally, breaking the heavy quiet. His voice was low and casual, but the tension in his shoulders betrayed more.

Mitch rotated his shoulder, his expression twisting. "They're getting bolder. We should move first before they think we're just sitting ducks."

Boomer shook his head. "If I make a move before the wedding, it'll put Jaz in more danger. And if Jaz is with Kalli, then Kalli will be in danger, too. That's what they want—me out in the open, swinging. They'll do anything to get the upper hand."

Nik let out a breath, flipping the folder closed. "Then we won't let them. The wedding's already a circus with this murder investigation. We'll keep an eye on the girls. Besides ..." He met our eyes. "Kalli and I are doing things our way now. Small. Private. Greek-mama defiance free."

Boomer snorted but didn't smile.

I flagged down the hotel café attendant and ordered chamomile tea then leaned back into the velvet chair cushion. I'd been sensing something building for days, but it hadn't snapped into focus yet. It was like watching a storm build offshore—silent but pulsing with electricity. Then, without warning, it hit me.

A subtle vibration in the air.

Goosebumps across my arms.

A cold drop of something sliding down the back of my neck.

I straightened. My heart started to race before my brain caught up. "Something's wrong," I said softly.

The lobby doors swung open with a gust of warm air.

A tall man in a black leather jacket walked in. He paused just inside, scanned the room like he was searching for a name on a list—slow, calculated. His gaze drifted over the front desk, the elevators, and the corner seating area before it landed squarely on Boomer.

My stomach dropped.

River, who'd been babbling only moments earlier, went completely still. His small fingers dug into Mitch's shirt. He looked up, wide-eyed, and whispered, "Bad." He was only twelve months, but he was already saying a few random words.

Mitch stiffened immediately. His protective instincts were always dialed to ten, but now? I could practically feel him readying for a fight.

"That's one of Ferraro's men," I whispered, low and even, to Nik. "I've seen him before in a vision. He's the one who watches. The one that tracks movement. He doesn't attack. He reports."

The man walked toward the café counter, pretending to inspect the pastries. He placed a coffee order, but his eyes never stayed on the menu. They kept drifting back. Watching Boomer. Calculating.

Tina looked up from her coloring, her eyes sparkling with curiosity. "Are we catching a bad guy, Daddy?"

Mitch reached over and gently ruffled her short, dark hair. "Not today, sweetheart."

Boomer's jaw tightened, and he never took his eyes off the man. "But soon."

The man finally accepted his cup of coffee and offered a nod that felt too casual. He glanced one last time at Boomer—lingering, deliberate—and then he turned and walked out the door.

I watched him leave through the window, but I could still feel his presence like a slimy residue in the room.

Nik let out a slow breath. "Think he'll report back to Ferraro?"

"Definitely," Boomer said. "They're keeping an eye

on me but obviously not ready to make a move yet. They're waiting for something."

I reached over and rested my hand gently on River's back.

He was still staring at the door, unmoving. He opened his mouth again, soft and ominous as he said, "Bang."

Just one word.

My heart stopped.

Bang.

Not loud, not panicked. Just ... certain.

I looked at Mitch, who immediately turned to Boomer. "They're not just looking for the drive. They're planning something."

Nik nodded. "They want leverage, probably."

Boomer looked over at us. "Even if they find the drive, they won't be done with me. I know too much. And now they think you all do too."

"First things first." I gathered my thoughts. "Didn't you guys send them on a wild goose chase?"

Boomer's mouth curled into a grim smile. "Oh yeah. And they're chasing it hard. We *hinted* at having the drive during a staged argument outside City Hall. We made sure word got around just enough."

"We fed the mamas just enough information, knowing word would get out. They know there's a drive, but they think top-secret wedding information is on it. Of course, they couldn't resist spilling the tea at their Thursday night Biriba Club," Nik said. "As expected, Despina told her cousin's manicurist that Boomer keeps a thumb drive hidden in a safety deposit box in Bristol. The mamas think Jaz is safeguarding it just like she is the ring. That'll keep them busy for a while."

"Sean, Cole, and I made sure to talk about files

with incriminating information at *Flannigan's Pub*," Mitch added with a half-smile. "We mentioned both Windsor and Bethlehem."

Nik nodded. "And we had Boomer make an appearance outside the county archives. That should send Ferraro's men running in several directions at once."

"They hit all three towns yesterday," Boomer said. "Ferraro's guys are sniffing around the Bristol bank like dogs after a bone, and someone broke into the historical records office last night in Windsor."

"They think the decoy drive is real," I murmured. "They think you actually have it, Boomer. What are they going to do when they find out you don't?"

Boomer's smile was grim. "We won't let that happen. There really is a drive out there. We just don't know for sure where it is. If Ferraro ever finds out I don't have it, he won't want any loose ends and we'll all be in danger."

"They'll stop chasing dead ends eventually," Mitch said.

"We just need the chase to continue until after the wedding," Nik replied. "Then we find a way to take him down and put him away for good even without the drive."

I looked back at the door again. The air still felt charged. River was calm now, back to playing with his dog's button eye. But I couldn't shake his whisper.

Bang.

Not if. When.

Nik stood and gathered the folder. "We follow Marcus next. Sunny, you said you had a vision."

I nodded. "He's paying someone off. I don't know who, but it's tied to one of his latest property deals."

Boomer looked at me. "And if Damon was involved?"

"Then that sounds like a good motive for murder to me," I said quietly.

We all went quiet.

Outside, the sun shone down on Clearview like it was just another peaceful day. But we knew better. A killer was still out there. The question was ... if we got any closer, would they kill again to keep us quiet?

9

KALLI

The parish center was supposed to feel peaceful. Serene, even. It had that polished wood floor smell, soft sunlight filtering through the windows, and the distant hum of Father Papadopoulos rehearsing Sunday's sermon in the church next door. But today?

It felt like a pressure cooker.

I sat at the long folding table near the windows, a giant binder of revised wedding plans in front of me. Vanessa sat across from me, her shoulders hunched, her blazer wrinkled in a way I'd never seen before. Her auburn hair was twisted into a messy bun, and deep circles clung to the skin beneath her eyes like bruises that wouldn't fade. The blood on her shirt had come back as hers, so she'd been released from jail and told not to leave town.

Everyone had been through so much, I had decided to give them all the benefit of doubt and still work with them until proven guilty.

Katerina and Effie were nearby, folding lavender napkins into perfect swan shapes like it was an Olympic sport.

Jaz arrived with her usual flair, balancing a

steaming to-go coffee in one hand and her leather-bound Maid of Honor notebook in the other. She dropped into the seat beside me with a groan.

"If I add one more duty to this thing," she said, flipping open the book, "it's going to qualify for a ZIP code."

Vanessa offered a tired smile, but it didn't reach her eyes.

"We're simplifying things, remember?" I told her gently, pointing to the checklist. "Smaller headcount. Single flower type. And I caved on Yiayia's almond cookies, so the Greek mamas can rest easy."

Vanessa nodded, but her fingers trembled slightly as she turned a page in the binder. Before I could say anything else, I spotted movement in the doorway.

Ozzy Finch.

He wore his usual janitor's coveralls and a frown like he'd swallowed something sour. He gave me a quick wave and jerked his head to the side. "Uh, Kalli? A sec?"

I excused myself and followed him into the hallway lined with framed parish photos and an old bulletin board with curling flyers.

Ozzy leaned in, speaking low. "I didn't want to bring this up in front of everyone, but ... I found something."

My stomach dipped. "Something?"

"In the room where Damon kept his photography gear. One of the maintenance crew was moving the old metal supply cabinet, and this must've fallen behind it." He handed me a photo sealed in a clear plastic sleeve.

I froze.

It was Vanessa.

In a hotel room. Her blouse was half unbuttoned,

and her arms were wrapped around a man whose face I didn't recognize—but I *knew* the body language. This wasn't professional. This wasn't platonic.

"This was in Damon's storage?" I asked, my voice tighter than I meant.

Ozzy nodded. "I figured the police missed it. Slid all the way under the cabinet. I didn't want to throw it away, not knowing ..."

"You did the right thing," I said quickly. My pulse thudded in my ears as I walked back into the main room.

Jaz looked up immediately. "What's wrong?"

I handed her the photo.

She let out a low whistle. "Oh boy."

Vanessa saw it in Jaz's hand and paled instantly. "Where did you get that?"

Jaz set it on the table in front of her, carefully, like it might explode.

"It was found in Damon's equipment room. Under a cabinet. It must have slipped out of wherever he was keeping it." I met her eyes. "Vanessa. Why did Damon have this?"

Vanessa stared at the photo, her lower lip trembling. She looked exhausted, not just physically but emotionally, like she hadn't taken a full breath in days. She pressed her palms flat on the table. "I didn't kill him."

"We're not saying you did," Jaz said carefully, "but it kind of seems like you lied to us."

Vanessa's face crumpled. "He was blackmailing me." The words dropped into the room like thunder. "I tried to get rid of the evidence, but he had copies. I should have known." She sighed.

Katerina gasped behind me.

Effie dropped a folded napkin.

Vanessa shook her head, her eyes glassy. "I was stupid. A few months ago, I had … an affair. It was one night. One *regrettable* night with a client. He was wealthy. Married. Important. Damon found out. He had photos of *that* photo shoot." She pointed weakly at the picture. "He said he would expose me. Ruin my career. He wanted money. And influence. I didn't know what else to do."

"Why didn't you go to the police?" I asked, my throat tight.

"Because I was trying to protect everything I built," she snapped, then immediately sagged. "I was desperate. I just wanted to get the photos and destroy them. That's why I went to the venue early. I thought maybe he'd left them in the storage room. I searched everywhere. That's how I scraped my arm. I never thought to look beneath the cabinet. I swear, I didn't know he was dead until Troy opened the trunk."

Jaz scoffed. "Why am I not surprised? That man collected secrets like they were limited-edition handbags. You weren't the first or the last."

Vanessa wiped at her face with the heel of her hand. "I didn't kill him," she said again, quieter, "but I hated him for what he did."

I didn't know what to say. I wanted to believe her. I *did*. But the timing. The secrecy. The way she'd crumbled now under pressure. It didn't feel like a coincidence. Before I could respond, the door flew open.

"I found you!"

It was Irene, my ever-determined baker. She was holding a manila envelope and a clear bakery box filled with six perfect mini cake samples. "Ophelia said you've been impossible to pin down lately, so I decided to bring the final samples to you."

I blinked at her. "You tracked me down through Ma?"

Irene grinned. "Greek mamas are like carrier pigeons with better aim." She looked around at the tension in the room, at the tears on Vanessa's cheeks, at the dropped photo still sitting in the center of the table. Her expression shifted quickly. "Is this a bad time?" she asked carefully.

Jaz slid the photo under a napkin. "Just a little drama. Cake might help."

Irene set the box down and handed me the envelope. "These are the final design options. You need to pick one soon so I can make sure I have the supplies."

I nodded mutely, still processing everything.

"I have to go." Vanessa stood shakily, clutching her purse. "Kalli ..." she looked at me, her eyes full of something between apology and exhaustion. "I didn't kill him. I promise you I'm telling the truth." Then she left.

Effie turned to Katerina. "Well, that explains the bags under her eyes."

Jaz lowered her voice for my ears only. "I think Damon had more tea to spill than we realized."

I looked at the door, where Vanessa had just vanished, and I couldn't shake the feeling Jaz was right. Because if Damon had blackmail material on Vanessa ...

Who else had he been holding secrets over?

Sunny

Sinfully Delicious always smelled like Heaven had gotten tired of being subtle and decided to open a bakery. The sweet scent of brown sugar, melted butter, and freshly brewed tea wrapped around me like a hug. Cozy string lights crisscrossed the ceiling, and the walls were painted a buttery yellow that made everyone look a little more alive.

I sat in the back corner booth by the window, a pot of herbal tea steaming in front of me, and River gurgling happily in the highchair at my side, his blond curls framing his angelic face. Across the street, I could see Kalli and Jaz through the big picture window at *Full Disclosure*. They were setting up new clothing displays in their spare time between wedding planning and investigating a murder.

Only in Clearview.

Boomer slid into the booth across from me, looking like he'd gone two rounds with a paper shredder and lost. His flannel shirt was wrinkled, his hair was tousled more than normal, and his eyes were shadowed with something heavier than exhaustion.

"Morning," I said gently.

He grunted in return.

Mitch followed, more put together but just as tense. He balanced a to-go coffee, a small plate of bacon cheddar biscuits, and Tina, who climbed into his lap the second he sat down. She plopped her detective book onto the table and flipped it open like a federal agent reviewing a case file.

"Daddy," she said in a whisper, "this one has magnifying glasses and footprints. That means *secrets*."

Mitch smiled, brushing her dark bangs out of her stormy gray eyes so like his. "That's very advanced investigative work."

Boomer stared down into his black coffee like it might reveal the answers to all life's problems. "Ferraro's men confronted me."

I blinked. "What?"

He nodded. "Cornered me at a gas station last night on the outskirts of town. Two of them this time."

Mitch froze mid-sip. "What happened?"

"They boxed me in. One stood by the pump, the other by the driver's door. Said they were done waiting. Told me if I didn't hand over the drive, there would be consequences and not just for me."

"Did they touch you?" Mitch's voice had dropped to that quiet, lethal level I knew too well.

"Tried," Boomer muttered. "Didn't go well for them."

"Are you hurt?" I asked, eyeing him.

"Bruised pride, and a sore shoulder." He lifted his arm halfway and winced.

Mitch swore under his breath.

Nik arrived a minute later, scanning the café before sliding in beside Boomer. He looked freshly showered but wired with anxiety, like someone who had too many tabs open in his brain.

"What happened?" he asked, his voice low.

Boomer filled him in.

Nik's hands curled into fists. "We need to tell the FBI that Ferraro is here."

"I'll handle that. I have history with them and this case," Boomer said. "But we need more than vague threats and parking lot brawls. Without the drive, we don't have proof of any of his illegal activities. Ferraro's smart. Everything flows through proxies and shell companies. No paper trail, no fingerprints."

Mitch scowled. "So, we're supposed to just wait until he makes a move that's not so harmless?"

"No," I said. "You make a move on him."

Tina flipped another page of her book and tapped her finger on a cartoon hound dog wearing a trench coat. "This one solves mysteries with her nose. Like River does."

River, completely oblivious to the rising tension, was babbling to his stuffed dog and laughing at a napkin that floated gently in front of him. Except there was no draft. No fan.

I blinked.

The napkin hovered, a delicate little drift, then began to swirl lazily in the air above his tray.

Tina caught it mid-air, tucked it under her book, and looked around like a squirrel hiding a nut. When her eyes met mine, she gave me an innocent, closed-mouth smile that said, *I saw nothing. You saw nothing. Right, Mommy?*

I shot her a wink and then sipped my tea as I reached over and brushed a hand through River's curls. "You've got to keep it subtle, little man," I whispered, more to myself than to him, worrying about how we were going to get through the terrible twos.

Boomer reached for his jacket to pull out his wallet at the same time that I reached for my tea, and my hand brushed the sleeve of the leather.

And just like that ... the world tilted.

A vision surged through me like ice water.

Boomer, stumbling backward into a narrow alley. A flash of fists. The glint of a knife. Blood spattering against concrete, dark and fast. Someone grunting. A hand gripping Boomer's collar as he fell, dazed.

I gasped softly. Just a breath—but enough.

Mitch glanced at me. "Sunny?"

I forced a smile and set my tea down. "It's hot. Just burned my tongue."

Lie, I told myself. Because sometimes, if you spoke a vision aloud, you rooted it in reality. And this one ...

this one I couldn't let be real. I needed to find a way to stop it before it ever happened.

Mitch's eyes narrowed as he studied me. My husband knew me well.

"I think you should trap them," I said suddenly, steering the conversation back on track.

Boomer looked up. "Trap who?"

"Ferraro's people. Obviously, what you've tried isn't working, so maybe it's time to change things up. Raise the stakes."

Nik arched a brow. "Risky."

"But smart," Mitch added. "We control the narrative. Choose the place, the timing. Set the stage for a showdown."

I nodded. "We plant the idea that they were right, and we purposely sent them on a wild goose. But Boomer had the real drive all along. He's hiding it. They'll chase *him* this time, and you'll be watching and waiting."

"We'll need convincing places for me to go. They'll follow me. I'm sure of it. I'll wear a wire this time. Get them to confess, then we'll have our proof. No drive necessary."

"That could work." Mitch nodded. "We just have to make sure someone is always backing you up."

Nik leaned forward. "We also need to keep Kalli and Jaz out of the crossfire. If they know the danger is this close, they will try to fix the situation like they always do. I can't risk either of their safety."

"Agreed—the fewer people involved, the better our chances of pulling this off," Mitch said, nodding.

River let out a squeal and clapped his hands, his sippy cup tipping over on its own.

Tina leaned into Mitch's chest and whispered, "Is trouble coming, Daddy?"

Mitch kissed the top of her head. "It'll be okay, princess."

Boomer's eyes drifted toward the window, to where Jaz was laughing at something Kalli said. "If Ferraro touches one hair on my wife's head ..."

"He won't," I said reassuringly. "Kalli's either." It wasn't their heads I was worried about. Inside, I was mentally mapping the alley. The one from my vision.

And praying I never saw it again.

10

KALLI

Final fitting.

It was supposed to be one of those magical moments—the kind you see in movies, with soft music, happy tears, and someone's auntie fainting gently at the sight of lace. Instead, I stood barefoot on a raised platform in the middle of my living room, pinned into layers of silk, while my seamstress looked like she was one wrong breath away from shattering.

Angela Reynolds had always been composed. Quiet, sure, but composed. She was the woman people called when their dress didn't fit the night before prom, or their mother needed a last-minute bustle stitched into her antique gown. Angela could thread a needle with her eyes closed and never once pricked your skin.

But today?

Her hands trembled so badly that I could feel it every time her fingers brushed the hem of my dress. She grumbled softly as she dropped a silver pin on the rug. It rolled under the coffee table, and she let it go.

"Everything okay?" I asked gently.

Angela didn't look up. "I'm fine," she snapped.

I blinked.

She caught herself instantly, pulling her hands back as if she'd just touched fire. "Oh my gosh—I'm sorry, Kalli. That came out wrong. I didn't mean to snap. I've just ... been having a tough couple of weeks."

"I understand," I said carefully. "You're not the only one."

Angela gave me a tight-lipped smile and turned back to the hem, but I couldn't shake the feeling crawling up my spine. The stiff set of her shoulders. The way she hadn't made eye contact with me once since arriving. Her whole presence was off.

I was about to press a little more when my phone buzzed from the windowsill.

Nik.

I glanced at Angela and she nodded it was okay for me to step away. I carefully stepped down from the platform, hiking the hem so I didn't trip over it, and grabbed the phone. "Hey." I walked across the room for privacy.

"Barry's equipment got trashed last night."

I froze. "What?"

"Someone broke into his trailer and destroyed most of his DJ gear. Smashed the main system, poured water into his backups. It's all toast."

"Is he okay?"

"Shaken. But yeah."

I ran a hand down my face. "First Damon's murder, now Barry's equipment. This can't be random."

"That's what I said," Nik replied. "It's starting to look like someone's targeting people connected to the wedding."

"Or to Damon." I looked over at Angela, who was now sitting very still on the couch, her hands folded in her lap like she didn't trust them to behave anymore.

"True," Nik continued. "Barry said he and Damon had a fight last month—nothing big, just drama about a couple events they worked together in the past that went south and who was to blame. Maybe whoever killed Damon has it out for anyone who worked with him."

"That's quite a list," I murmured, not sure I was convinced. "This incident might be completely unrelated to the murder. Sunny had said the murder felt deeply personal, with the murderer directing their rage specifically at Damon. Not at some event gone wrong and all the people connected to it."

"Noted. We're keeping our eyes on all possibilities. I'll come by later to check in on you, Ballas."

"Thanks, Detective," I said teasingly, adding softly, "I could use it."

No sooner had I hung up than the front door flew open and Jaz burst in like a gust of thunderstorm winds. "I come bearing a pick me up!" She held a bag of snacks and the leashes of Chanel and Versace, who immediately hit the floor and pranced into the room like they owned the place.

Behind her, Wolfgang let out a long sigh from his corner. He took one look at the newcomers and dropped his head back onto his oversized paw with the world-weariness of a male who'd seen too much.

"The puppies are still at training class?" I asked.

"Yes," Jaz said, brushing her caramel waves out of her face. "Willow decided she didn't want to obey a single command. Meanwhile, Armani sat on the instructor and refused to move. They called it 'gentle defiance.' I call it a vibe."

Chanel and Versace barked once—loudly—and locked eyes on Prissy, who was perched regally on the windowsill like a very offended queen.

"Uh-oh," I said.

Prissy narrowed her eyes.

Versace whined, and Chanel barked again.

Then all Hades broke loose.

Prissy bolted across the room, an orange, black, and white blur of fury and fluff on her tail. The poodles followed, yipping gleefully, all flying ears and jingling collars. Wolfgang decided his nap was over and it was time to play.

"NO!" Jaz and I shouted in unison.

Angela yelped and ducked as they tore past, knocking into her sewing kit. Pins scattered like confetti across the floor.

Prissy zigzagged through the living room, then the dining room, until she launched herself onto the table. It was set up with wedding accessories—veil, jewelry, bouquet mockups ... and my shoes.

My *wedding* shoes.

Delicate, ivory, imported satin heels with hand-stitched lace and tiny pearl embellishments, custom-dyed to match a swatch of Ma's wedding dress. Limited edition. Artisan made. And the most beautiful shoes I had ever owned.

With a final burst of cat vengeance, Prissy kicked the box off the table with both back feet. It landed on the hardwood with a dramatic *thud*. One shoe bounced upright. The other? Straight into Wolfgang's water bowl.

I stared at it, horrified.

Jaz covered her mouth with both hands. "Kalli ... I'm so sorry. But you have to admit, that was kind of iconic." She rushed over and let the dogs out back.

Angela scrambled to her feet, rushing over to grab the waterlogged shoe with shaking fingers. "I can clean it," she whispered. "I'll get it reshaped. Re-dyed. I can ... I can fix it."

Her voice cracked on the last word.

She wasn't talking about the shoe anymore.

I crouched down beside her, my dress bunched awkwardly around my knees, and touched her arm. "Angela," I said softly, "something's going on. You're shaking. You've been on edge since you walked in. Talk to me."

She looked at me for a long moment, her eyes rimmed red. *I didn't think anyone knew.*

"What does someone know?" I asked softly. "What do they have on you?"

She blinked, staring at me a little confused.

"Your face says it all," I clarified, not wanting her to know I heard her thoughts.

Her hands tightened around the shoe and she sighed, her shoulders falling in resignation. "Damon had something on me. Information I'm not proud of from years ago—before I opened my own shop."

I sat quietly listening.

She swallowed hard and then continued, "I spread false information about the head seamstress where I worked. She lost most of her clients. Then when I opened my own shop, I reached out to them. That's how I built my clientele."

I still said nothing, keeping my face free from judgement.

She shook her head, her face flushing with embarrassment. "I was young. Stupid. Insecure back then. I thought it was behind me. Damon found out and threatened to reveal what I had done to everyone. He said he would ruin me if I didn't help him."

"Help him how?" I asked.

"Promote him. Talk him up to clients. Send business his way. I became a big success because of those initial clients and worked with some pretty big names since then. Damon knew that. He wanted to use me. Name-drop me. I hated it, but I supposed it was karma catching up to me. I wanted to scream, but I was scared. I don't have a husband or children. All I have is my business. If this got out—"

I squeezed her hand. "Angela. Did you—"

"No," she said quickly, but didn't think any thoughts to verify her answer. She pulled her hand away. "I didn't kill him. I wanted the proof gone. That was all. I searched his office and, admittedly, the parish center storage room. I thought maybe I could find the evidence. Steal it back, but ... I never got the chance."

I nodded slowly, my heart pounding. It made sense. It *fit*. Angela wasn't the first. Vanessa had been blackmailed too. And if Damon was threatening vendors one by one ... who else had he cornered?

Jaz crouched beside me, the poodles now back inside and lying innocently at her feet like they hadn't just orchestrated a household coup. "What did I miss?"

"Another secret. Another victim of Damon's," I said.

Angela wiped her eyes and looked at me. "I didn't mean to fall apart today. I just ... the fitting, the dress, the wedding—I wanted this to be perfect for you."

"You're doing everything right," I said. "I promise. We all made mistakes in the past. Your work speaks for itself now."

Angela rose slowly, cradling the soggy shoe like a broken promise. "I'll take care of this. You don't need to worry."

But I did worry.

Because the more we peeled back Damon's life, the more it looked like a spiderweb—with people like Angela, Barry, and Vanessa all tangled in the center. And if someone had snapped?

While I didn't condone murder, I could understand how they might lose control.

Sunny

Lila Cross's house looked like a Pinterest board gone stale—faux-lavender wreath on the front door, matching porch cushions slightly faded by the sun, a decorative chalkboard that read *Grateful, Thankful, Blessed* in curling script. The flower boxes were dry, the porch steps needed repainting, and every curtain was drawn tight like the house was trying to hide something.

Kalli and I stood at the edge of the walkway. Neither of us moved right away.

"You sure you want me here?" I asked.

Kalli nodded, her mouth pressed in a thin line. "I don't trust Lila. She has already lied once."

I followed Kalli up the steps, the air thick with tension.

The door opened before we knocked. Lila leaned against the frame, her arms crossed and eyebrows already raised. She looked tired—but not the sleepless-mom kind of tired. This was bone-deep, soul-worn exhaustion. Her makeup was a little too perfect, her lipstick freshly applied, but her eyes were dull.

"Kalli," she said, her voice flat. "And psychic sidekick. Lovely."

"Good to see you, too, Lila," I said, sweet as syrup.

Kalli didn't bother with pleasantries. "We came to ask about Damon's business. Troy says you're selling it to him."

Lila shrugged and stepped back, motioning for us to come in. The inside of the house was cooler, clean but impersonal—like she'd scrubbed it raw to keep the past out.

"He made me an offer," she said, heading into the kitchen. "I accepted."

"You believe him?" Kalli asked, trailing behind her. "That selling to Troy is what Damon wanted?"

"Troy said as much. I have no reason to believe he would lie to me. He never has before," Lila replied. She poured herself a glass of iced tea and didn't offer us any. "They worked together. Damon trusted him."

Kalli crossed her arms. "No, he didn't. Damon was going to fire him. He told me that the week before he died."

I bit back a smile. More like Kalli had heard Troy's thoughts.

Lila froze for a heartbeat over Kalli's comment. Then she sipped her tea and walked to the window like the conversation didn't matter. "Well, it's not like it makes a difference now." She shrugged.

"You're selling him something he doesn't deserve," Kalli said.

"Damon didn't care about *me*," Lila snapped, spinning around. "He stopped caring a long time ago. He only cared about my family's money and demanded more alimony from me. He gutted my accounts. Left me digging through couch cushions for coins while he posed for magazine spreads. So, forgive me if I'm not sobbing over his legacy."

There it was. Beneath the calm, beneath the

makeup and the perfect lip color, was a deep-seeded bitterness she could no longer hide.

"I don't want the business," she continued. "I want the money. The only thing Damon left me that doesn't come with a guilt trip or a legal threat."

"I'm not judging," I said gently. "Are you sure you want to give up what is rightfully yours? I doubt you'll ever get what it's worth from Troy."

Lila laughed. It wasn't joyful. "If I could afford to, I would give it away for free just to make Damon roll over in his grave. Try living in a house full of photo prints of women he barely knew, smiling in wedding gowns while your own marriage is rotting under your feet." Her voice cracked on the last word. She cleared her throat, suddenly self-conscious, and turned toward the hallway.

"I'm sorry," Kalli said with a softer tone. "That must have been difficult."

"I have a call in five. So, unless this is leading somewhere ..."

Kalli's jaw tensed. "I guess we're done then."

Lila walked us to the door in silence and shut it after we stepped out.

On the porch, I paused. A scarf lay draped over the wicker chair, patterned with swirls of burgundy and gold. It fluttered slightly in the breeze, catching my eye. I reached out and brushed my fingers along the fabric.

And everything around me fell away.

Lila's hand trembled as she twisted the cap off a pill bottle in a bathroom lined with marble. A wineglass sat on the counter. It wasn't empty. Her eyes were glassy in the mirror. Smudged mascara. She flinched at a knock on the door.

"Don't make me come in there," Damon's voice called.

She closed her eyes, trying to breathe.

"I swear, Lila," his voice came again, sharper, crueler. "If you don't get it together, I'll take the kids. You'll lose everything."

She spun, slamming her hand against the wall.

"I'll tell the judge," he growled. "I'll destroy you."

Then a while later, Lila and Damon stood outside this very house—screaming. Her voice was ragged, his calm and cold. She lunged for his camera bag. He shoved her back.

"You think I won't expose you?" he barked. "You think I won't show them all? I keep pictures of everything on everyone."

Lila stumbled. Then stared. Her mouth opened, but no words came.

The vision snapped back into the present with a painful jolt. I staggered, catching myself against the porch railing.

Kalli grabbed my arm. "You okay?"

I nodded, blinking fast. "Just a little dizzy." *She isn't broke just because Damon demanded more alimony. She's an addict.*

Kalli's eyes widened as she let go of my arm and we stepped down the front walk in silence. That was when a voice called from the next porch over.

"Nosy question, but are you two asking about Damon?"

We turned.

It was the neighbor—an older woman in a floral house dress and slippers, watering her petunias.

"I saw him here," she said casually, like she was talking about garbage pickup. "Last week. Him and Lila were screaming at each other on the porch. Loud. Real nasty. Good thing their little ones are with their

Nanna for a couple weeks. I was gonna call the cops, but they stopped before I could dial."

Kalli exchanged a look with me.

"Thank you," I said.

She waved us off. "Just saying. People think because she's quiet now that she wasn't angry then. She was angry, all right. Said she wished he was dead."

We kept walking.

At the car, Kalli leaned against the hood. "She lied. Again."

"She's scared," I said. "Not innocent. But scared."

"What did you see?"

I hesitated. I thought about the pill bottle. The wineglass. The way Lila had looked at herself in the mirror—empty and fractured. "She's been struggling for a long time," I said finally. "Damon knew. He used it against her. Threatened to take the kids. Said he would ruin her. And he had proof in pictures. Proof of a lot of people in pictures."

Kalli didn't speak for a moment. Then, she responded softly, "If you push someone far enough ..."

"They push back." I looked up at the house again.

Lila had shut the door behind her, but something told me the past was still inside. Waiting. And it wasn't done speaking.

11

KALLI

I never thought I'd get an invitation to the infamous Thursday night Biriba Club without a hidden catch—like being guilt-tripped into it or bribed with souvlaki. But here I was, standing outside Despina *Lambros Yarn and Card Shop* with Sunny, holding a box of koulourakia and a bottle of pome-granate soda, wondering what level of chaos waited behind the door.

"You ready for this?" Sunny asked, glancing side-ways at me with a grin.

She was wearing her signature flowing kimono top and silver earrings shaped like crescent moons. Some-how, she always looked like she'd just stepped out of a dream and had all the answers. I, on the other hand, was nervously adjusting the strap of my crossbody bag like it held classified secrets.

"Ready as I'll ever be," I said. "If I survive the gossip and the card slaps, I'm calling it a win."

Jaz was working late. Jo and Zoe were at the hotel, exhausted from the kids. And Sunny's mother, Vivian, claimed a headache, but we all knew the drama from the Greek mamas was a bit too much for her. She'd offered to watch her grandkids so Mitch could help the guys with the investigation and Sunny could join me.

The Trio had insisted on making their own grand entrance earlier.

Sunny and I stepped inside, and I was immediately enveloped by the scent of lavender sachets and freshly brewed Greek coffee. The shop was warm and humming with chatter. Yarn cubbies had been pushed to the edges of the room, replaced with a long folding table draped in an ivory lace tablecloth.

The usual neat order of the store was gone, and chaos reigned in the best way possible.

"Ah, look who decide to grace us!" Ma called out from her seat near the window, fanning herself with a deck of oversized cards. Her black hair was piled high in its usual beehive, and her eyes sparkled with mischief.

"She late," Chloe added, scooting over to make room. "I already shuffle twice."

"She forgiven," Aunt Tasoula chimed in, her nails clicking against the rim of her coffee cup. "They bring pastries."

"That buys you five minutes of mercy," Despina said from behind the counter, where she was pouring glasses of soumada with the air of someone mixing potions.

I offered the box of cookies like a peace offering. "Wendy's out sick, but Sunny and I brought reinforcements."

"Poor thing," Despina said, clucking her tongue. "Did she eat from that sushi truck again? That thing is a lawsuit waiting to happen. Raw fish and tropical fruit—what kind of barbarianism is that?"

Sunny chuckled as she settled into the seat beside

me. "She's resting. Said to tell you all to play nice, though I'm not sure she meant it."

With the cards dealt and the snacks within arm's reach, we began what quickly devolved into a battle of theatrics and false modesty.

"I play for fun," Ma declared, laying down a perfect meld of queens.

"Oh sure." Chloe snorted. "Just like you 'accidentally' win church raffle three years in a row."

"The gods work in mysterious ways." Aunt Tasoula made the sign of the cross.

Deserving an Oscar or not, their competitive energy was contagious. Sunny and I tried to hold our own, but we were clearly the underdogs. I laid down a set of eights with pride, only to be met with a slow clap from Aunt Tasoula.

"So brave," she said dryly.

"This game makes me feel like I'm twelve again, sneaking cookies and eavesdropping," I whispered to Sunny as Despina reshuffled the deck. The laughter and banter in the room felt like a live-wire—messy, loud, and weirdly comforting.

"I have to admit, it's a nice distraction. Thanks for including me. You're doing great, by the way," she whispered back. "You only got called 'child' once."

The banter slowed only long enough to make room for gossip, which flowed more freely than the Ouzo.

"Tasoula's grandson got tattoo. On his *neck*. It's a *flame*, like little fire demon." Ma shook her head.

"He's an artist, no?" Despina asked.

"He a dasher, whatever that is." Aunt Tasoula shrugged. "I no understand young people speak."

"Maybe he's one of those modern artists," Fiona said after a sip of Ouzo and a wink. "You know, dash around with no clothes on to capture the human form. It's called figurative art."

"I'm sure you *figured* you'd try it out." Granny Gert rolled her eyes, then sipped her drink with a wince, fanning her face.

"You figured wrong. I don't dash, darling. I glide." Fiona patted her red hair.

"Well, you're both wrong," Great Grandma Tootsie said, taking a sip of the rye and ginger she'd brought along with her from the hotel. "Even I know a dasher is someone who delivers food to your door. Pure laziness if you ask me. People need to learn how to cook. Boys oh day, no one can take care of themselves these days."

"He deliver *fire,* apparently," Aunt Tasoula muttered. "Barely out of high school and already ladies' man."

Ma grunted. "My Jasper no ladies' man. Still no find nice Greek girl. I hoping at Kalliope's reception ... if there ever is one."

Chloe leaned forward like she was sharing nuclear codes, changing the subject, thank Zeus. "Did you hear? Marina caught her husband texting someone named 'Plumbing Angel'? At midnight."

"Maybe he have leak," Ma offered.

"Yeah," Aunt Tasoula deadpanned. "I have leak too. I blame the Ouzo and the babies."

When the laughter died down and another hand began, I took a moment to excuse myself, heading over to the yarn shelves under the pretense of admiring skeins of soft baby alpaca blends. The truth? I needed a break. The joy was real, but my nerves were fraying. I was supposed to be wedding planning, not mingling while my fiancé chased leads. And I still hadn't heard from my biological father. What if something hap-

pened to him and he wasn't able to reach me? His sabbatical was pretty remote.

I was starting to get worried.

Sunny wandered over with her cup of tea and
leaned on the yarn shelf beside me. "Color therapy?"
she asked, eyeing a ball of blush-pink merino wool I
hadn't realized I was squeezing like a stress ball.

"Something like that."

Then we both heard it—low voices floating from
behind the counter. The Greek mamas weren't being
nearly as discreet as they thought.

"I saw her do it myself," Tasoula whispered. "Jaz
tuck it right into lining of sparkly clutch."

"She safeguarding both," Chloe added. "The ring
and the drive."

"What drive?" Ma asked, her voice low and con-
spiratorial. "The one with *secret wedding plans?*"

I blinked. My mouth parted as confusion scrambled my brain like eggs in a hot pan.

"What secret wedding plans?" I whispered to
Sunny. "What drive? What are they talking about?"

She straightened a little too quickly, blinking at me
with what was definitely a guilty smile. "Maybe a
backup of your Pinterest boards?"

I narrowed my eyes. "Sunny."

She gave me a wide-eyed shrug. "I have no idea.
Maybe Jaz just wanted to keep all your hard work safe.
You *did* say you weren't having the wedding until
after—"

"After Damon's murder is solved," I finished. Because that was the truth. I couldn't plan a wedding
with a body in a trunk and half my vendors looking
suspicious. It felt wrong.

Sunny reached over and nudged me lightly with
her shoulder. "They're just trying to help. You know

them. If they're whispering, it's probably about table-cloths or adding tzatziki stations." *At least I hope that's all. We don't need to worry about them, too.* She quickly straightened as if realizing she was still touching me.

"With drives?" I asked, wondering who was the *we* and who else were they worrying about?

"I'm sure it's nothing more than they love secrets and can't stand that they're not in on one."

I sighed. "I just don't like feeling like the bride that everyone's planning around."

Sunny grabbed the yarn I was squeezing to death, her fingers brushing mine. *More like they think you're the one with secret plans you stored on a drive for safe keeping.* She pressed her lips together, wincing.

"Where in Mount Olympus did they get that idea from?"

She blinked and let go of the yarn. "Oh, look! The break's over. Let's go." She quickly led the way back to the table.

We sat down just in time for Despina to announce, "The next round will be called The Redemption of Kalli. Let's see if she can play one hand without violating international card law."

I raised an eyebrow. "I'll have you know I studied for this."

Ma smirked. "Did you also practice losing gracefully?"

"Oh, I'm great at losing. I just make it look like a dramatic plot twist."

"You mama raise you right." Aunt Tasoula nodded.

Everyone laughed—even Despina, who was already dealing like a Vegas pro. And as I looked around the table—at the women who had shaped my childhood and the new friends who filled my adulthood—I felt at peace. Maybe, just maybe, this mess of a pre-wedding was the perfect prelude to the actual one. I narrowed my eyes with determination.

But that didn't mean I wasn't going to figure out what secrets were hiding in Jaz's purse.

Sunny

The heat shimmered off the sidewalk like invisible waves as Zoe adjusted the shade on baby Alannah's stroller, and I wiped River's forehead with a damp cloth. He'd already gone through two popsicles, a corn dog, and at least three complaints about his "sticky neck."

Tina was flitting through the grass with a flower wand, pretending she was summoning sun sprites.

Clearview Park was bursting with life.

The Summer Solstice Festival was one of the biggest events of the year. Booths lined the paved paths, decorated with sunflowers, ivy garlands, glittery wind chimes, and little chalkboard signs offering everything from kombucha on tap to "solstice intention readings."

It reminded me of home.

My mother was in her glory shopping with the trio, while my father was having a grand time playing checkers with Kalli's pop, papou, and Aunt Tasoula's man Hank.

Behind me, Jo was once again wrangling the twins, who were currently deep in a debate about whether a caterpillar could beat a raccoon in a fight. Tina was chiming in to settle the argument by stating if the caterpillar was magic like River, he could. That started a whole new debate on magic.

Zoe pushed baby Alannah's stroller back and forth, soothing her. "If I don't eat an entire funnel cake in the next twenty minutes, I might start hallucinating."

"I already am," I muttered, blinking toward the dunk tank where someone was taunting kids like a carnival pro.

But what really caught my eye was the *Full Disclosure* booth.

Kalli and Jaz were in their element—set up beneath a canopy adorned with gold tassels and eucalyptus wreaths, their matching "Let Your Internal Beauty Shine on the Outside" t-shirts looking spectacular against the elegant lavender bunting behind them. Kalli was arranging her *Kalli Original* lingerie while Jaz was setting out the newest trendy summer fashion pieces. People lined up around the booth, admiring and buying various pieces.

Then I spotted them.

The Greek mamas.

Ophelia and Tasoula had just emerged from their adjacent booths—*Aphrodite's* and *Hera's Halo*—where they'd spent the last hour alternately handing out food samples and inspecting people's looks. The two joined the third mama, Chloe. They looked over at Kalli and Jaz, bending their heads together in secret conversation—never a good sign according to Kalli— then they started to move.

They were moving in a cluster, walking briskly but with an air of forced nonchalance that immediately raised red flags. They weren't talking loudly. They weren't sipping frappes. They weren't correcting anyone's posture.

They were up to something.

I watched them veer off the main path, toward the

old locker bank near the edge of the rec center. These lockers were originally meant for lifeguards back when *Clearview Park* had a pool, long since drained and converted into a wildflower garden, according to the brochure at the Historical Society's booth.

A whisper of dread slid down my spine.

"Hey Zoe? Jo?" I turned to face my friends. "Can you take the kids to get ice cream? Like ... right now."

Zoe raised an eyebrow. "Uh, sure. Is something wrong?"

"Just ... a hunch. Psychic stuff."

Jo didn't even flinch. "You want soft serve or swirl?"

"Surprise me."

With a nod, they herded the kids toward the concession booths, and I slipped off the path and quietly followed the mamas. I stayed low, using the string of hanging plants and the canvas wall of a henna tent for cover. When I rounded the corner of the locker building, I stopped short at the scene before me.

They were *definitely* trying to pick the locks.

Tasoula had a bobby pin in her mouth, and she held a compact mirror angled toward the latch. While Ophelia was on her knees, elbow-deep in one of the bottom lockers with a paring knife.

I blinked. "Okay. That's new," I whispered to myself.

Chloe was keeping a lookout like she was guarding the crown jewels, fanning herself and muttering, "Hurry, someone going to come. Or worse—Jaz going to show up."

They must've heard the rumors the detectives had started. All was going according to plan, but breaking into the lockers wasn't anticipated.

I stilled when I sensed movement.

Out of the corner of my eye, beyond the lockers, in

the shadow of the old maintenance shed—I saw them. Two men. Lurking. Wearing polos and mirrored sunglasses. One leaned against the wall like he had all the time in the world. The other held a phone and tapped his fingers on the screen without looking away from the mamas.

Ferraro's men.

They weren't just watching the booth anymore. They were following the mamas. Oh God. I crouched down and immediately called Mitch.

He answered on the second ring. "Hey, Tink."

"Mitch," I whispered, ducking behind the rose bush near the lockers. "*Clearview Park*. Ferraro's guys are here. They're watching the *mamas*. You need to get here. Now."

"We're close," he said. "Nik and Boomer are with me. Stay put."

Less than five minutes later, the familiar trio appeared—Mitch, Nik, and Boomer all walking with purpose and barely concealed annoyance. But by the time they reached the locker bank, Ferraro's men were gone. Slipped away like shadows.

Mitch scanned the area, his jaw tense. "They were here?"

"Yes. Watching them." I pointed at the mamas, who had just managed to wedge a locker open. "They're following *them* now."

Boomer let out a low whistle. "They're getting bold. I really thought they would follow me, but you know how rumors go. They change. Too many versions of what could be on the drive are out there now."

"Which makes controlling the narrative that much more difficult." Mitch clenched his jaw with a worried look I knew well.

"Captain Crenshaw and the mayor aren't going to

like this one bit," Nik muttered, then stepped out of the shadows as he took in the scene before him. "Did we interrupt a heist?"

The mamas jumped. Tasoula immediately dropped the mirror. Ophelia straightened like a guilty cat, holding her now bent paring knife. Chloe blinked rapidly like a hummingbird hovering, ready to fly away at any second.

"We just—uh—checking locker air quality," Ophelia said brightly. "Humidity cause mold. That no good. Very bad."

"Sure," Boomer replied. "And I sunbathe in parking garages."

"Why you do that?" Tasoula's face puckered. "No wonder you pale boy."

I just shook my head.

"We want little peek," Chloe admitted. "At the drive. You know, the one with you secret wedding plans?"

Nik sighed. "There are no secret plans, Ma."

"Well," Chloe huffed. "You been so secret lately. How we *not* supposed to be suspicious?"

Mitch frowned. "Ladies, we don't know anything about a drive, but you can't go picking locks in public parks like criminals."

"And you especially can't do it while being tailed by *actual* criminals," Boomer added.

The mamas froze.

"Criminals?" Ophelia squeaked. "Like The *God*father?" She made the sign of the cross.

"Yes," Mitch said flatly. "So back to your booths. Please."

Grumbling, adjusting their shawls and dignity, the mamas retreated. I could still hear Chloe muttering about "cement shoes" as they walked away.

"This is getting dangerous," Boomer said.

"Agreed." Mitch's brow furrowed. "They think the mamas have the drive now."

Nik's jaw hardened. "They're desperate."

"Yeah, but Kalli's not dumb," I said. "She's asking questions. She's starting to get suspicious."

Boomer glanced over his shoulder, his lips tight. "We need to wrap this up before the wedding turns into a war zone."

Nik nodded, his face pinched. "Kalli can't take any more drama. I'm afraid she really will call off the wedding if she finds out about this."

"Well, we need to do something before innocent people get hurt," Mitch added.

My stomach turned over as I remembered my vision. I wasn't so worried about the innocent people right now. Ferraro's men might not be following Boomer yet, but they would be. And I was afraid he was definitely going to get hurt.

It was time I told Mitch about what I saw.

12

KALLI

When I asked Jaz to come with me to *Razor's Edge Weapons and Outdoor Supply* store, I didn't expect her to dress like we were going to Coachella. Aviator sunglasses, a linen blouse knotted at the waist, and lip gloss that caught the sunlight like a beacon.

"I can't believe we're doing this," she muttered, swinging her iced coffee like a talisman as we crossed the parking lot. "This is so exciting." Her brow puckered. "Although, so many murder podcasts start this way."

"Relax. We're not actually *buying* a knife—we're just asking about them," I said, adjusting my ponytail instead of my usual chignon, and smoothing my hands over my t-shirt and jeans.

I had purposely dressed casually and different from my normal in case anyone was watching. I'd thought Jaz intuitively knew to do the same. Apparently not, or she just didn't care if people gossiped. I, on the other hand, didn't need the mamas giving me a lecture on owning weapons of any kind.

"Speak for yourself. I just might buy a taser." She

grinned. "Gotta keep Boomer on his toes now that we're married."

I rolled my eyes and laughed. "You're so bad," I said as I pushed open the door to *Razor's Edge*.

A tiny bell chimed overhead, announcing us like sirens at a crime scene.

Inside, the air was cool and sharp with the scent of gun oil, metal, and rubber. It reminded me of a hardware store, if the hardware was all designed to kill something. Blades gleamed from behind glass display cases, hanging from pegboards and locked behind steel mesh. Everything from pocketknives to survival blades, combat-style hunting tools, and even ornate daggers with dragon hilts, according to the signs.

A man behind the counter looked up. He was built like an ex-biker—gray beard, denim vest, eyes like steel. The kind of guy who probably read survivalist forums for fun.

"Well," he said, cracking a grin, "look what the law dragged in. Detective Stevens's girl and her wing woman."

Jaz offered a slow blink. "You may address me as her glamor queen, thank you."

I gave him a polite smile. "We're not here to shop, Mr. Lawson. Just here for information."

He leaned his arms on the glass counter, his expression tightening. "This about that dude who got himself killed? Damon?"

I nodded. "I'm sure you heard he was stabbed."

"Town's been buzzing. People never used to get murdered in Clearview. They overdosed, crashed fourwheelers, or ran off with their yoga instructor. These days murder seems to be happening far too often." His voice softened slightly. "Shame. Damon didn't seem like a bad guy. Just a little too ambitious. Always poking his nose into other people's business."

"Which might be what got him killed," I said.

Lawson exhaled through his teeth, nodding, and then tapped the glass. "What are you looking for exactly?"

"The murder weapon hasn't been found, and I don't really have many details," I said, having no idea what the puncture wounds had looked like. Nik wasn't sharing much with me these days. He didn't want me to stress about anything, but keeping me out of the investigation only stressed me out more.

Merle nodded, already opening a binder and flipping through purchase slips like it was routine. "Could be a lot of blades. I told your fiancé the same thing. Hunting, tactical, even an old Ka-Bar. Connecticut law says you can carry a knife with a blade under four inches without a permit. Anything bigger, you better have a good reason."

"So switchblades?" Jaz asked, sipping her coffee.

"Illegal to carry. Still sold, though," he said, flipping another page. "Collectors. Defense. You'd be surprised what people justify."

I leaned closer to the counter, watching as he scanned entries. "Have any locals picked up anything concerning lately?"

He paused, tapping a name. "Barry Franklin. Big into antiques. Comes in every couple weeks to browse or talk shop. Bought a nineteenth-century Italian stiletto replica a while back. Not practical. Sharp, though."

I jotted the name down. Barry had been on our radar, especially after his DJ equipment had been trashed. And we knew he and Damon had worked a gig that went south. There was definitely animosity between them.

"And this one," Lawson continued, tapping another slip, "Troy Bennett. He comes in here a lot. Bought a Benchmade switchblade about three weeks ago. Black grip. Push-button release. He was adamant he needed it for protection."

I blinked. "Troy carries a switchblade?"

"Claims it's for self-defense," Lawson said. "But he didn't strike me as the type who knows how to use it."

Jaz raised an eyebrow. "And yet, he's suddenly armed and edgy."

I was about to ask more when the front door chimed behind us and in walked Troy himself, wearing faded jeans and a Red Sox T-shirt. He paused the second he saw us. His eyes flicked from me to Jaz to Lawson, reading the vibe like a man who just walked into his own intervention.

"Well," he said, stuffing his hands into his pockets, "I can't say I expected to see you two here. Are you following me?" He was growing bolder, no longer intimidated by us like he had been at the beginning of the investigation.

Or he was getting a little too comfortable.

Jaz smirked. "In your dreams, Red."

I stepped forward. "Actually, Troy, we were just talking about you."

His eyebrows lifted. "Should I be worried?" Some of his bravado slipped.

"That depends. You still carrying that knife you bought?" Jaz arched a brow.

He hesitated then pulled a set of keys from his pocket and jingled them. "Nope. Left it at home today. Why?"

I hesitated for a second. Nik was going to kill me

for divulging any information, but we were running out of time, and I needed answers. "Because Damon was stabbed," I said. "And we're looking into anyone with a weapon that fits the description."

His expression turned frustrated. "You think I killed him?"

"I think you fought with him." Jaz stepped closer to him. "In public. Loudly."

I fought a grin. I loved seeing Jaz work her magic.

Troy looked genuinely worried for a second, then he blew out a breath. "Yeah. We fought. But not over anything that would make me kill him. Damon was my boss. He got in over his head. I warned him."

I frowned. "Warned him about what?"

He hesitated. "Marcus."

"Marcus?" Jaz asked.

Troy rubbed the back of his neck. "Look ... I overheard Damon telling Marcus he knew about him paying off zoning officials. Backdoor deals for land permits. Clearview properties. Construction projects."

My stomach tightened. That was motive. And it painted a whole new picture. "He was blackmailing Marcus?" I asked.

"I don't know the details," Troy said. "But Damon had something. Documents. Audio, maybe. Enough to scare Marcus. Next thing you know, Damon's telling me people are following him."

Jaz's gaze met mine before she asked, "What kind of people?"

"Muscle," Troy said grimly. "Guys in suits. Clean-cut. The kind who don't look like they belong in Clearview."

"Hitmen?" I whispered.

He shrugged. "I don't know what they were exactly, but I do know that was the only time I ever saw

Damon nervous. Really nervous. Said they came right up to him. Told him to back off or else."

"And now he's dead," Jaz said quietly.

Troy looked at us, his eyes sincere. "Look, I don't know everything. But you're barking up the wrong tree if you think I had anything to do with it. If I wanted Damon dead, I wouldn't have tried to convince him to go to the cops."

I wasn't sure what to believe. He had lied about Damon wanting to make him partner, but was he actually capable of murder? "Thanks for the info," I said, my voice low.

As Troy left clearly frustrated, without getting anything or even talking to the owner, Jaz turned to me, her brows knit. "So. Barry collects knives, Troy carries one, and now we've got Marcus caught up in bribery and threats."

"The kind of men he described would definitely carry knives," I murmured.

We stood in the middle of the weapons store, surrounded by gleaming steel, yet I didn't feel protected in the least. Marcus's words that someday Damon was going to push someone too far came back to me. He had known things he shouldn't, and now we did too. Weapons didn't always protect you from the people watching in the shadows.

And we were getting close enough to feel their breath.

_____

Sunny

It wasn't the lakeside getaway Jaz had originally planned—there were no spa robes or bonfire singalongs or Instagram-perfect charcuterie boards on dockside platters—but *Flannigan's Pub*, warm with low amber lights and smelling of beer, wood smoke, and old varnish, had its own kind of magic.

Jaz had outdone herself. Pink and gold streamers looped overhead, and a handmade banner that read *"Kalli's Last Stand"* in glittered cardstock hung crookedly over our table. A "Bride To Be" sash rested in Kalli's lap like she wasn't sure she wanted to wear it, and fake engagement ring drink charms clinked against glasses filled with everything from merlot to mocktails.

We had taken over the long wooden table in the back corner of *Flannigan's*—the one under the stained-glass light shaped like a shamrock. It was loud, a little chaotic, and absolutely perfect.

"Well, this isn't exactly a weekend in flannel pajamas and wine-fueled honesty circles," Kalli said, twirling her straw in her drink, "but I love it. Thanks, Jaz."

"You're very welcome. Given the circumstances, I think I rocked it." She winked, lifting her glass and taking a sip.

Kalli smiled at that, but there was an edge behind it. The laughter at the table—the overlapping conversations, the clinking glasses, the mix of my Divinity girls with her Clearview crew—didn't erase the unease that hung just under the surface.

"Okay," Jo said, raising her shot glass, "here's to the bride. May your wedding be beautiful, your husband competent, and your in-laws not too involved."

"Cheers!" we chorused.

I sipped my diet cola—designated psychic and sober support system—and let the warm hum of voices drift around me. Jo, of course, had taken command of the drinks like she was back behind the bar at *Smokey Jo's*. She was currently trying to convince Leni, Kalli's waitress cousin, to try her homemade habanero-infused whiskey next time she was in Divinity.

Zoe was talking centerpiece strategy with Zena, the calm and collected bartender girlfriend of Silas. And Winnie, Kosmos's mail carrier girlfriend, was gently teasing Nik's cousin Thalia about her recent courtroom theatrics.

"I only yelled because he deserved it," Thalia said matter-of-factly. "No one lies about being allergic to bees *and* asks for extra honey in their tea."

"You should've seen her in heels chasing him down the courthouse steps," my cousin Leni added proudly.

It was fun. I let out a deep exhale. A moment that felt almost normal, if you didn't look too hard at the edges.

Kalli leaned toward me, her voice lower now, intimate in the way that meant she'd been waiting for the right moment. "With all this crime drama, I forgot to tell you. Guess what the mamas did last week."

"Please tell me it doesn't involve setting someone's hair on fire with incense," I said.

"Close." She grinned. "They showed up at *Full Disclosure* first. Marched in with a canvas tote full of lemons and glass evil eyes. Claimed they felt a disturbance in my aura. Then they came to my house and performed full-on protection rituals."

I blinked. "All of them?"

"Ma, Chloe, and Aunt Tasoula. They salted every corner of my living room, taped garlic cloves over my front door, sprinkled holy water on my sofa—and then Ma lit something in a pan and said it was an old priest recipe. I'm pretty sure she nearly summoned the ghost of her papou."

"At least they didn't recruit my mother or The Tasty Trio." I laughed and then sobered. "The mamas are worried," I added carefully.

She gave me a look. "You think?"

"More than usual," I amended.

Kalli took a slow sip of her chardonnay. "They said it's because 'The *Gods*father' was following them after they broke into the lockers at the park. Cronus is a destructive, all-devouring god." She studied me as she spoke. "They were looking for the mythical wedding drive, so now they think the wedding is cursed."

I tried not to flinch.

"I asked Nik about it," she continued. "And he confirmed a couple of men were following them, not gods, but then he totally brushed it off. Said it was nothing. Just a coincidence. But they followed them, Sunny. Through the park. Into the parking lot. I think someone is after them."

I widened my eyes, feigning surprise, but couldn't bring myself to speak.

Kalli's tone shifted, from amused to something harder. Something more worried. "I know you know something," she said softly. "Was it the same men the guys had issues with in Atlantic City? Some thug from Boomer's past?"

I stared at her for a second too long. Then I shrugged, playing neutral. "I don't know for sure." Liar. I hated lying to her. But I'd promised Mitch and the others not to say anything—especially not now, not when things were building.

"It can't be. Boomer told me Ferraro wasn't in Clearview. I'm sure it was someone else, like Marcus's thugs." Jaz leaned across the table, clearly overhearing us.

My stomach turned sour. They were going to be so angry when they found out the truth.

"We've been thinking," Jaz went on. "What if Damon *did* hide something in those lockers before he died? It sounds like he had dirt on a lot of people."

Zena perked up. "What kind of something would he hide?"

Winnie tilted her head. "Marcus has thugs?"

"Evidence," Jaz said. "Troy told us Damon had dirt on Marcus. Something about bribes and zoning permits. And Marcus sicked some thugs on him to scare him."

"Real estate corruption?" Thalia asked, immediately alert. "That's felony territory."

"And if Marcus found out Damon was blackmailing him," Kalli said, "it could be motive. Real motive. Either he or his thugs could have killed him."

Zoe frowned. "But if that's true ... and Damon hid something ... that would mean whoever was watching the mamas was trying to get to it too."

"Exactly," Kalli said. "The mamas thought the drive was a wedding plan, but maybe it was evidence of Damon's dirt all along."

I sat frozen for a moment, my fingers curled around my glass.

If Damon had slipped something into those lockers, something real, then the decoy became dangerous. Because now Ferraro's people might be looking in the right place for the wrong reason, and innocent people might actually get hurt for real. This whole mess was spiraling out of control.

The pub door creaked open.

A breeze rolled in, and two men stepped inside.

Tall. Clean-cut. One wore a blazer too sharp for a Saturday night. The other had slicked-back hair and mirrored sunglasses—indoors. They scanned the room casually, but with a precision I recognized all too well.

Kalli saw them.

So did Jaz. And her expression shifted instantly from amused to razor-focused. "Those guys," Jaz said under her breath. "They match Troy's description."

Kalli nodded. "The ones who threatened Damon."

"And the ones who followed the mamas?" Zena asked.

No one answered. We just watched them take a booth in the corner. Not too close. But definitely within view.

"I don't like this," Zoe murmured, her party planner vibe giving way to full-blown mom energy. "We're not safe if they're still hovering."

"Do we leave?" Winnie asked, glancing among us.

Kalli sat back, crossing her arms. "No. We're not giving up the table. Not for them."

"Agreed," Jaz said.

I looked at my friend, glowing in the pub lights, surrounded by people who loved her—and who, at this rate, might all end up collateral damage if the detectives didn't take down Ferraro soon.

I smiled a little too bright and changed the subject. "Okay. Who wants to do bachelorette trivia?"

Jo slapped the table. "Bring it."

Thalia grinned. "You're all going down."

We launched into questions and laughter and mock arguments, but the awareness never left. Those men were still watching. Still waiting. And Damon's secrets had nothing to do with what was on the real drive. The decoy might've been fake, but the danger?

That was very, very real.

13

KALLI

The sun was warm, the kind of golden soft light that made the sidewalks feel like heated stone and the storefront awnings ripple in the breeze. Summer in Clearview always smelled like fresh-cut grass, waffle cones, and sunscreen.

Wolfgang lumbered at my side like the furry mountain he was, sniffing flowerpots and letting out the occasional thunderous snort. Willow, the fluffy Saint Berdoodle with more energy than a toddler on pixie sticks, zig-zagged across the sidewalk like she had an invisible to-do list.

Nik walked beside me, sunglasses perched on his head, the leash handles looped around his strong hand like he wasn't tethered to two dogs the size of a small horse and a miniature pony. His free hand occasionally brushed mine, grounding me without even trying, and making me smile over his wayward thoughts.

I tugged at my tank top and sighed. "You know what I learned last night?"

"That glitter stays on everything forever?" he offered.

"That too. But mostly, that my friends are dangerous when given an open bar and trivia cards."

He laughed. "Tell me everything."

I smiled, letting the warmth of the memory buffer the weird tension still buzzing beneath my ribs. "Jaz turned *Flannigan's Pub* into bachelorette boot camp," I said. "There were games. Custom drinks. Zoe made a glitter board where everyone wrote their favorite thing about me—except Jo just wrote 'hot' six times."

"She's not wrong," Nik murmured.

I grinned, nudging him. "It was loud and messy and perfect. But then—" My voice caught.

Nik glanced at me, his head tilted.

I exhaled. "Two men came in late. Tall. Clean-cut. One had a navy blazer that practically screamed 'I make shady deals at Irish pubs.' They looked exactly like the guys Troy described—the ones who cornered Damon before he died."

Nik's steps slowed just a little.

"I swear, Nik. It wasn't just coincidence. Jaz thinks they're the same men who followed the mamas after they broke into those lockers at the park."

We passed Aunt Tasoula's *Hera's Halo*, the scent of hair dye and lilac shampoo drifting onto the sidewalk. Across the street, a little boy tried to balance an ice cream cone taller than his face while his grandmother hovered nearby like a tiny, anxious hawk.

Nik didn't answer right away. He just gave Wolfgang's leash a tug when the dog tried to nose into someone's planter box.

I frowned. "Nik," I finally said. "What are you thinking?"

He didn't look at me. "I think you shouldn't go anywhere alone right now."

I blinked. "That's not an answer."

He stopped walking.

I turned to face him, my heart already thudding with the weight of everything unsaid.

"I'm not trying to shut you out," he said quietly. "But whoever killed Damon is a real person and still out there. I can't protect you if you're chasing down every clue with Jaz and Sunny."

"I'm not helpless," I snapped, unable to hide my frustration. He had been acting strange for a while now. Like there was something he wasn't telling me. We were supposed to be getting married at some point. There shouldn't be any secrets between us.

"I know you're not helpless," he said gently. "Believe me, I *know* that. But you are human, and you're not a cop. I've seen what this kind of thing does to people who think they're untouchable." His voice cracked, just slightly. Enough for me to see the way his hand tightened on the leash like it might anchor him to something solid.

"What aren't you telling me?" I asked softly.

He hesitated.

"Is it Ferraro's men?" I whispered.

He exhaled. "I don't want you worrying more than you already are."

Too late. The worry was already living beneath my chest as my heart began to pound.

Before I could say more, Willow let out a little bark and veered toward a patch of shade. That's when I saw her ...

Lila Cross.

She was stepping out of the narrow alleyway behind *Wilma's Wine and Spirits*, adjusting her designer sunglasses and smoothing down her crisp white blouse. She looked too put-together for an alley exit. Too glossy. Too perfectly perfumed.

My instincts tingled.

And then—seconds later—a tall woman emerged from the same alley, heading in the opposite direction. She had slicked-back black hair, a blazer that fit like it was sewn on by angels, and heels that probably cost more than my Prius. She moved like a woman used to owning every room.

Nik saw her too. His posture shifted just slightly, his eyes tracking her movements like a trained hawk.

"Who in Hades is *that*?" I breathed. Clearview was a small town, but lots of people hung around after the Summer Solstice Festival had ended.

"No idea," he said. "But she doesn't look like she came for a pedicure."

"Come on," I muttered, already crossing the street.

We caught up with Lila just as she was pulling out her phone and pretending not to notice us.

"Lila," I called, my voice bright and falsely casual.

She jumped a little and then turned with a tight smile. "Hello, Kalli. Detective."

"Afternoon stroll?" I asked.

"Oh, I just finished at Wilma's Wine and Spirits," she said. "Stocking up for summer parties. You know."

My gaze ran over her. "Did you forget your bags?"

"I host a lot of parties," she said without missing a beat. "Wilma is gracious enough to deliver my order."

Last I'd heard she was broke, but then I remembered she'd pawned something at *Nelson's Jewelry Store* a while back. I glanced at the alley behind her. "Interesting way to exit."

"The back door," she said too quickly. "Traffic's terrible up front today."

Nik stayed silent, letting me take the lead, putting his keen observation skills to work.

"I couldn't help but notice you talking to someone back there."

Lila blinked. "Who?"

"The woman who left just after you. Fancy shoes. Corporate dragon energy."

"Oh," she said, and her smile slipped. "Her. She just asked for directions."

"In the alley?"

"She was ... confused."

"What's her name?"

Lila hesitated for a beat too long. "I didn't catch it. She was just ... a sales rep, I think. Avon? Or something. Totally harmless."

Avon sales didn't buy clothes like that, I thought.

Nik shifted beside me. I could feel his energy sharpen, but he still said nothing.

"Well," I said. "If she was harmless, why not use the front door?"

Lila laughed, a high-pitched sound that reached Mount Olympus. "Honestly, I didn't think anyone would notice. It's a long alleyway. You have no proof we left the same building."

"We tend to notice things," I said. "Especially when they involve mysterious women slinking through alleys in heels."

Lila's lips tightened. "If I see her again, I'll let you know."

"Please do."

We let her go, watching her walk off a little too fast, a little too stiff.

I turned to Nik. "That woman wasn't selling Avon."

"Nope."

"She knew Lila."

"Yep."

"And Lila was *scared* of being caught."

Nik nodded. "But she also didn't panic. Which means this wasn't her first back-alley meeting."

We stood there in the street, watching traffic pass, people stroll, laughter drift from open restaurant patios. And yet—beneath all of it—something darker hummed.

"She's involved in this," I said. "Maybe not the murder, but something."

Nik's jaw flexed. "I agree. But until we know more, we can't go accusing a perfect stranger of anything."

"I suppose not." I sighed as I looked back down the alley, where secrets had passed hands behind the liquor store in the middle of a sunny afternoon. I might not be able to accuse Mystery Woman, but that didn't mean I couldn't look into her.

Sunny

The sun was still high when we pulled up to Wendy's flower shop, which was in the back of her house, though the breeze had just enough cool in it to promise a pleasant evening. Her house sat at the edge of town, just before the winding road turned into the hills. It was one of those cozy old colonials with pale blue shutters and a wraparound porch filled with flowerpots in mid-bloom.

Out back, her greenhouse stood like a glass cathedral—domed and glowing in the light, practically humming with life.

Wendy met us at the front steps, her apron streaked with pollen and her gray and brown hair pinned up with a pencil. She looked better—rosier, lighter on her feet—but there were still traces of fatigue under her eyes.

"Look who decided to grace me with her presence," she teased, wiping her hands on her apron as we filed in.

Kalli grinned. "We come bearing decisions."

"About time," Wendy said. "I was starting to worry I'd have to pick your wedding flowers myself. You'd end up with thistles and drama."

"Well, I already have enough drama," Kalli muttered. "But I could do without thistles."

Jaz waved a hand. "They're too spiky. Symbolic, sure—but they don't exactly say, 'please sit quietly and enjoy the ceremony.'"

Wendy laughed and ushered us inside, and we stepped into what could only be described as a living floral fairytale. Every inch of the shop was bursting with color—bundles of wildflowers in jars, roses in soft creams and vivid reds, eucalyptus bunches strung like garlands. The air was heady with scent, sweet and herbal all at once.

"Feeling better?" Jo asked gently, trailing behind me as we fanned out.

Wendy nodded. "Much better. Whatever it was, it passed. I just needed rest—and chamomile tea and a break from Biriba Club gossip."

"Blasphemy," Zoe said, mock offended.

"I know. The mamas probably thought I was dying," Wendy said with a smile. "Ophelia left a Tupperware of lemon rice and a note that just said, 'Be strong. Survive.'"

We laughed, but Wendy's eyes grew distant for a moment. She touched the edge of a teacup on the display shelf, turning it absently.

"Just been thinking about ... old things lately," she

said quietly. "Missing Ben. We had a tiny wedding. Backyard. Barefoot. He picked my bouquet himself— sunflowers and baby's breath. Said they were 'unfussy, like me.'"

Silence settled around us like petals.

"I didn't know him," I said gently, "but Ma says you always light up when you talk about him, and she was right."

"He made ordinary days feel sacred," Wendy said. "And now, most of the people who knew me then—my parents, my sister—they're all gone."

Zoe wrapped an arm around her shoulders. "I'm so sorry, Wendy."

She nodded, blinking fast. "My sister ... she left this earth way too soon." She didn't say more. And none of us pushed. There was a tremor in her voice that didn't need translation. Something awful had happened to her.

Kalli, ever tactful, cleared her throat. "Well. Speaking of bouquets—today's the day."

Wendy smiled, her face slowly brightening again. "Then let's make it count."

We spent the next hour narrowing Kalli's options for her more simplistic wedding from five to three to one. We all had opinions—Jo liked the wildflower blend, Zoe pushed for classic peonies, and Jaz said if the bouquet didn't have meaning, it didn't belong at the altar.

But in the end, it was Kalli who picked the mix of lavender, cream roses, and olive branches. "Simple, but symbolic," she said, holding the sample arrangement in her arms like it was sacred. "Peace, clarity, strength."

"I love it," Wendy said, and I could see it in her

eyes—this mattered to her. Being part of something joyful again.

Afterward, we headed to *Rosalita's Place*, a Southwestern-style Mexican restaurant tucked just outside the center of town. It was far enough from the Greek strongholds to avoid running into the mamas or Kalli and Nik's extended families, and Kalli swore by its cleanliness.

"I went to high school with Rosalita," she explained as we took our booth near the back. "She was the only person in Home Ec who cleaned the stove before and after using it. You *bet* I trust her kitchen." She still pulled a little bottle of hand sanitizer from her purse and wiped down her silverware, just in case. Kalli being Kalli.

The restaurant was warm and golden, with clay walls, wrought iron lanterns, and chili peppers strung in the windows like festive warning signs. The scent of chipotle and fresh lime lingered in the air, and a mariachi cover of "Dancing Queen" played softly from the speakers.

"So," Zoe said once our orders were in, "let's talk wedding. You've simplified things?"

"Very." Kalli nodded. "Intimate ceremony. Outdoor reception. One dress. One man. Three pets. No fire breathers or ice sculptures."

"And only *some* Greek dancing?" Jo asked.

"Depends on how much ouzo shows up uninvited," Jaz replied.

Laughter bubbled around the table.

Then Kalli's expression shifted. "I need to tell you something," she said, lowering her voice. "Earlier today, I told Nik about the men at the bachelorette party who looked like the guys Troy described. He's acting so secretive. I got suspicious and asked him if the men could be Ferraro's."

I swallowed hard, trying to act nonchalant. "What did he say?"

"He didn't. He told me he didn't want me to worry, and then we got distracted when Damon's ex-wife Lila came out of the back behind the liquor store. She met with a tall mystery woman as fancy as herself, Gucci bag, stilettos, and all. Lila claimed the woman was a stranger asking for directions. Said she was selling *Avon*, of all things."

Jo snorted. "With a Gucci bag and stilettos? Not likely."

"Exactly," Kalli agreed. "And I don't believe for a second it was a chance encounter."

I had been sipping my tea, but the tight swirl of energy in my chest had been building since we entered. Like something in the atmosphere didn't want to be ignored. "I'm gonna run to the bathroom," I said, standing. "Be right back."

The hallway to the restrooms was dim and cooler than the dining room, lined with southwestern pottery and desert-themed art. As I reached for the women's door, it opened from the inside. And *she* stepped out. A fancy woman with a Gucci bag and stilettos.

The mystery woman.

Tall. Poised. Hair like black lacquer. A faint perfume trailed her—gardenia, heavy and sweet with a bitter afterbite. Her sunglasses were still on, though the hallway was dark, and her expression was unreadable.

We brushed shoulders as we passed. Just a moment of contact.

And the world *shifted*.

The restaurant blurred.

I was no longer standing in the hallway but some-where colder, darker—an apartment, unfamiliar and ster-ile. A hand reached across a table, sliding a black velvet pouch to Lila. Her nails trembled as she took it.

Barry appeared next, laughing—but the sound was wrong. Nervous. Hollow. A flash of the mystery woman's face, impassive, cold. A whisper: "No loose ends."

Then—a man's voice. Not Damon's. Someone else's. "He knew too much."

The vision jolted again.

Three figures in shadows. A deal. A warning. Money exchanging hands. The mystery woman stepped away ... like a queen leaving a chessboard after declaring checkmate.

I gasped, the world snapping back around me in a cold rush of air and fluorescent buzz.

I gripped the sink, breathing hard. The cold porce-lain grounded me. I splashed water on my face, staring into the mirror.

They're connected. Lila. Barry. The mystery woman. But it wasn't *Avon.* It was something far more intense.

By the time I returned to the table, the food had arrived—fajitas sizzling, tortilla chips overflowing, bowls of salsa balanced precariously.

"You okay?" Zoe asked, reading my face imme-diately.

I sat down, still pale, and leaned in. "She's here. Mystery Woman. I saw her. In the hallway by the re-strooms. She brushed past me, and I had a vision."

The table went still.

"What did you see?" Kalli asked quietly.

"Lila was receiving something from her," I said, keeping my voice low. "A small velvet pouch."

Jo's forehead pinched. "Jewelry?"

"Possibly, but that wasn't all. Barry was there. They

were all involved in something. There was money and talk of someone knowing too much."

Kalli went rigid. "Damon."

I nodded. "And whoever this woman is, she's at the center of it."

Jaz looked toward the back of the restaurant. "She's gone now?"

"She was leaving as I went in," I said. "But she's still *here*. Somewhere. I can feel it."

Jaz straightened, her hand instinctively brushing her purse where she kept her taser. We all scanned the restaurant and sucked in a breath when we spotted the back corner of the room.

Barry was sitting there. At a small table. With *her*.

The woman with the sleek black hair and icy smile. She looked even more polished now that I had a chance to study her—like danger dressed in designer labels.

"Speak of the devil," Zoe murmured.

"No," I said, staring hard as the pieces inched closer to connecting. "Speak of something far scarier."

14

KALLI

The morning air smelled like fresh-cut grass and the faint scent of cinnamon rolls baking. Jaz and I made our way from *Full Disclosure* across the street to *Sinfully Delicious*, the little stone-front building with frosted windows and a pink neon sign that said *Sin a Little*. It was practically our church service for the non-holy: caffeine, gossip, and pastries.

We rarely started our day without it.

When we pushed open the door, the sweet scent of baking cinnamon rolls and vanilla frosting hit us like a full-body hug. The warm buzz of conversation and clinking coffee cups filled the cozy space.

Maria was behind the counter today, wiping down trays with one hand and popping a bite of something into her mouth with the other. She waved the rag in greeting. "Morning, troublemakers," she said, grinning.

"Morning," Jaz chirped. "The usual, please—caffeine, sugar, and something so sinful it should require confession."

I laughed. "And I'll take the organic bran muffin and an herbal tea."

Maria chuckled as she reached for a paper bag.

"You know you're ruining my brand with that muffin, right? I only make these for you."

"And I appreciate that," I said sweetly. "Besides, someone has to balance Jaz's sugar spiral."

As Maria prepared our order, Irene was visible through the little kitchen window at the back, hunched over a three-tiered wedding cake like it was a science project. The smell of almond paste and fondant drifted out with every opening and closing of the swinging door.

"You know," Maria said, leaning over the counter conspiratorially, "Irene's been crazy busy. Seems like everyone's getting married this summer."

I nodded. "Wedding season."

"Yeah, well, not all is blissful," Maria said, dropping her voice lower. "There's been a string of thefts. Wedding guests are getting their jewelry and wallets stolen right off tables at receptions."

Jaz leaned in so fast she almost knocked her pastry onto the floor. "Seriously? I heard about that last year, but I thought it had died down and wasn't a problem anymore. I can't believe it's happening again this year."

Maria nodded. "Yep. Small stuff mostly. A gold bracelet here. A couple designer wallets there. Enough that it's getting the rumor mill talking."

My mind immediately went to the mystery woman we'd seen with Lila and Barry—the one who radiated secrets and bad intentions like she wore them under her perfume. "You don't think ..." I said slowly.

Jaz's eyes widened. "That it's her?"

Maria frowned. "Who?"

"Long story," I said quickly. "Tell us more about the thefts."

Maria shrugged. "All I know is it's been happening

at the bigger venues. Nobody catches anything on camera. Whoever it is, they're good at blending in."

"And Barry's been DJing at a lot of those," Jaz added.

Maria wiped her hands on her apron. "Speaking of Barry, you might be interested to know I overheard him and his assistant arguing the other day. Josh was pretty worked up. Said he wasn't going to do 'it' anymore."

"It?" I echoed.

Maria shook her head. "Didn't hear what 'it' was. Just that Barry told him to get his act together, and Josh stormed out."

Jaz's face lit up. "You are a treasure trove of shady tidbits this morning."

"I live to serve," Maria said, handing over our bagged-up orders.

As we turned toward the door, I spotted Boomer tucked into the corner near the fireplace with a cup of black coffee. Across from him was Ozzy, leaning in close for a low conversation.

I nudged Jaz. "Boomer sighting at two o'clock."

"What's my husband doing with Ozzy?" She arched an eyebrow.

We exchanged a look that said, *This is too interesting to ignore* and then casually wandered over.

Ozzy spotted us first and gave a polite smile. "Morning, ladies."

"Morning, Ozzy," I said, trying to sound breezy. "Big plans today?"

"Just heading to the church," he said, pushing up from the table. "Got a lot of clean-up to do after the last wedding."

"Hard to keep up with all the candles and flower petals," Jaz said, smiling.

He chuckled. "You'd be surprised." He tipped his hat and made his way out, leaving his half-empty coffee behind.

Boomer leaned back in his chair and gave us a look like he knew exactly why we'd wandered over. "Did you order pastries," he said dryly, shooting a mock scowl at his wife, "or were you planning to steal mine?"

"We heard you have a lead," I said without missing a beat, sitting down across from him. Jaz smirked as she plopped into the chair beside me, balancing her latte and pastry.

Boomer sighed like a man who knew resistance was futile. "There's been a break."

I leaned in. "Tell me everything." With Nik absent, I might actually learn something useful.

"I'm sure Nik told you," he said, lowering his voice, "the murder weapon wasn't a knife."

I blinked. "What?"

He cursed under his breath. "Your fiancé really needs to do a better job of letting me know what I can and can't say."

"Too late now," Jaz said around a mouthful of pastry. "Out with it, babe."

He sighed. "It was scissors."

Jaz choked on her latte. "Scissors?"

"Not sure what kind of scissors," Boomer clarified, "but sharp enough to puncture deeply. Clean entry wounds. No jagged tears like a standard knife would've made."

I sat back, trying to picture it. Somehow it felt more personal, more improvisational. A crime of opportunity or desperation. "And Ozzy?" I asked.

Boomer nodded. "Ozzy told us he saw Vanessa—the wedding planner—with a pair of heavy-duty utility scissors in her event kit the day Damon was found. Said she always carries them for cutting ribbon and stubborn floral foam."

"Any other leads?" I asked, my heart picking up speed.

Boomer nodded again. "Angela had sewing scissors. Kept them on her rolling cart when she was at the church."

"So two people with scissors ..." Jaz said, trailing off. "And two very different motives."

"Lila has children who love arts and crafts that utilize scissors, and she is in a scrapbooking club." Boomer finished his coffee and pushed the cup aside. "We're looking into all possibilities. I mean, let's face it. Most people have scissors of some sort. And the killer could have used someone else's scissors. But it means Damon could've been killed with something grabbed in the heat of the moment. Doesn't exactly scream premeditated."

"But whoever did it still made sure he was hidden," I said quietly. "Still made sure someone else took the fall."

Boomer's eyes softened. "We're getting closer."

I looked over at the bakery counter where Irene was piping buttercream onto a wedding cake and Maria was refilling coffee cups. Here they were worried about thefts at the weddings, completely unaware of the deeper cracks running under our town's surface.

Boomer threw down some cash for a tip, then his forehead creased with worry lines as he gave us each a parting look. "Keep your eyes open and be careful. The streets of Clearview are more dangerous than ever."

We promised we would. As Jaz and I stepped back into the sunlight, the bag with our pastries swinging at my side, I couldn't help but feel like the noose was tightening. Not just around the killer. Around *all of us.* I was more determined than ever to risk danger and find the killer because whatever was coming next ... it wasn't going to be as easy to cut away as a piece of ribbon at a wedding.

It was going to bleed.

Sunny

The sky was a watercolor blue, a few lazy clouds smeared across it like someone had forgotten to finish the painting. The playground behind the *Clearview Hotel* was a little sun-bleached, a little squeaky, but it was fenced in and shaded by a giant oak tree that turned the whole area into a dappled mosaic of gold and green.

Our picnic blanket was a cheerful disaster. Half sandwiches, juice boxes, baby wipes, and crumbs spread between three exhausted couples and a handful of children who seemed to think they were starring in their own high-octane action movie.

"Detective Tina Stone is on the case!" Tina shouted, brandishing a magnifying glass bigger than her face.

She marched a circle around the playground, her pink cowboy boots kicking up little puffs of dust. River, playing in the grass next to the swings, was flicking dandelions into the air without touching them, using nothing but his mind.

I caught it out of the corner of my eye—the swing creaked as it moved, though the air was perfectly still. No breeze. No nudge. Just River's concentration and that faint buzz of invisible energy he didn't quite know how to rein in yet.

I glanced around. We were alone, thank goodness.

I leaned over and whispered, "River. Honey. *Subtle.*"

He grinned at me with his first baby teeth on display and let out an ear-piercing squeal, startling baby Alannah from her slumber in the stroller next to him. Zoe picked her up when she began to cry.

"Mom, can I be the bad guy?" Collin asked Jo, his face streaked with chocolate.

"No, *I'm* the bad guy!" Jeremiah yelled, shoving his brother lightly.

Jo sighed, handing a bottle of water to her husband Cole. "They've been fighting about who gets to be the villain since breakfast."

"Parenting goals," Zoe said, bouncing Alannah gently on her shoulder. The tiny girl wore a floppy sunhat and a sleepy smile that made everyone's heart melt a little.

Mitch sprawled next to me, arms folded behind his head, sunglasses on, looking every bit the relaxed dad enjoying his Sunday. But I knew him better than that. His cop radar was still pinging, especially after everything I'd dumped on him last night.

After my vision.

Nik and Boomer had split off that morning to follow their own leads, but not before slipping Mitch a photo one of the hotel desk clerks had snapped. Mystery Woman was staying here at the *Clearview Hotel.* Charming the staff, slipping through hallways, leaving nothing but perfume and speculation behind.

Mitch had immediately done some digging.

"So," I said, stretching out on the blanket beside him. "You going to tell me what you found out?"

He turned his head slightly, lowering his voice so only I could hear. "Used a few connections from my NYPD days."

"And?"

"Vivienne Noire," he said, drawing out the name like it tasted bad. "She's the real deal. Real wealthy. Real powerful. Real secretive."

"What kind of business is she in?" I asked, curious.

"That's the thing," Mitch said. "No one knows exactly. Real estate, consulting, private acquisitions. High-end clients all up and down the East Coast. She moves money, buys companies, flips assets. Quietly. Legally, mostly. But there's a reason no one's sure what else she deals in." He sat up a little, watching the kids through his sunglasses. "She's a ghost when she wants to be. Leaves no fingerprints. She has a lot of friends in high places—and probably a few in very low ones."

"And Barry's cozying up to her," I murmured.

"And Lila," Mitch added grimly.

I wrapped my arms around my knees, feeling the early summer sun warm my skin even as a chill snuck under it. Vivienne Noire wasn't some random socialite looking for Avon sales. She was *dangerous*. The kind of dangerous that didn't need to shout to be heard.

Tina raced back to the blanket, dropping her magnifying glass onto the cooler with a thunk. "I have new evidence!" she announced proudly. "The bad guy eats ALL the cookies!"

Jeremiah and Collin immediately started wrestling again, shouting about cookie rights and jurisdiction.

Zoe snorted, shaking her head. "At least they're keeping it nonlethal."

"Today," Jo muttered.

River stood on wobbly legs and walked over to me, pink-cheeked, with energy buzzing just beneath his skin. He had a twinkle in his eye, which made me think the little devil knew exactly what he was doing —pushing swings, nudging balls, sending sand flying with a twitch of his fingers.

It scared me sometimes. How visible it was becoming. How easy it would be for someone to notice if they were paying the wrong kind of attention. I kissed the top of his messy hair and passed him a juice pouch. "Good job being careful, bud."

He beamed at me, much smarter than the average one-year-old, but then again, he wasn't your *average* toddler.

Mitch's phone buzzed quietly against the blanket. He picked it up, glanced at it, then frowned.

"What?" I asked.

"Nik. Says they're trying to trace where Vivienne's been staying before she showed up here. But she uses aliases. Fake names. Even fake charity foundations."

"She's hiding something," I said.

"No question," Mitch said, sliding the phone back into his pocket.

"But what?" I whispered, looking out at the playground. Everything looked so normal. So bright and sunny and *safe*. But under the surface, something sharp was waiting.

The kids barreled back over to us when Zoe opened a Tupperware of cookies, the playground instantly abandoned in favor of chocolate chip diplomacy.

We spent another hour lounging, laughing, stealing bites of each other's sandwiches, and swapping old stories—trying to pretend, if only for a little while, that the shadows creeping closer to our lives didn't exist. But they did. And somewhere, probably within walking distance, Vivienne Noire was plotting her next move.

When it was time to pack up, Mitch and I loaded the stroller while Tina helped River buckle his sandals.

Jo waved a half-eaten apple slice in the air. "Tomorrow night. Girls' night at *Flannigan's*. No murder talk, no weddings, no weird visions."

I smiled. "I'll believe that when I see it."

"We'll tie you to a barstool if we have to," Zoe promised.

As we headed back into the hotel, I caught a glimpse of a sleek black car parked at the far end of the lot. Windows tinted. License plates from out of state. A sliver of movement behind the glass—just enough to make my stomach tighten.

I didn't need a vision to tell me Vivienne Noire was still watching. Waiting. Planning her next move. I had bumped into her. And now we were asking around about her. She was smart. Savvy. And the real question was, what exactly would that move be?

15

KALLI

By ten-thirty, Jaz and I had *Full Disclosure* gleaming—candles flickering on every windowsill, sunlight showcasing the latest display racks, and essential oils making the air smell like lavender had thrown a very classy party. We even had a fresh pot of herbal tea steeping behind the counter, just waiting for the first lull.

For approximately fifteen seconds, it was perfect.

Then the front bell jingled—and chaos marched in wearing orthopedic sandals and an over-application of Chanel No. 5.

"Girls! We here!" Ma bellowed like we hadn't just seen each other at church on Sunday.

Behind her Aunt Tasoula adjusted her sunglasses even though we were inside, and Chloe carried a tray of homemade pastries. Trailing behind them like colorful parade floats marched the infamous Tasty Trio: Granny Gert, Fiona, and Great Grandma Tootsie.

Jaz visibly braced herself, her coffee halfway to her lips. "This is happening," she whispered. "And we are powerless to stop it."

I straightened my blouse, pasted on my most diplomatic smile, and prepared for impact.

"Kalimera, my beautiful girls!" Ma cried, sweeping me into a floral-scented hug that nearly knocked me off balance. *You too skinny. Poor Nikos gonna starve.*

"Good morning to you, too," I squeaked and then stepped back out of her embrace. I didn't need to hear any more of her thoughts about my skills—or lack thereof—as wife material. I was already stressed enough that I wouldn't be any good.

Aunt Tasoula was already tutting and reaching for my hair. "You need more volume, Kalliope. You flat like pancake. I fix. Okay? Okay."

I dodged her embrace. "Actually, I prefer it this way."

"*You* need better eyeliner, Tasoula," Fiona tsked, waving a wrinkled hand. "You look like a raccoon who lost a fight."

"I *destroy* you in smokey eye contest," Aunt Tasoula snapped back.

Chloe, meanwhile, slammed a giant plastic tub onto the checkout counter. "Spanakopita!" she declared. "Eat before you waste away like deflated balloon. You need big hips to give me lots of grandbabies."

Not to be outdone, Granny Gert produced a paper sack with a flourish. "Cookies! Gluten-free! Tweedle dee! You're welcome, children!"

And Tootsie—Zeus bless her—yanked out a silver flask and waved it proudly. "What's coffee without a little Irish whisky? For bravery, boys oh day."

At this point, Jaz had silently retreated behind the jewelry display, peeking out with the expression of a woman watching a wildfire from behind a glass door.

Sunny drifted in last, looking like she desperately regretted her life choices. She gave me a pained smile that said: *I tried to stop them. I failed. Forgive me.*

The boutique, which was meant to be a calming oasis of self-indulgence, now buzzed like a market-place in Athens at rush hour.

"Where's Vivian?" I asked.

"She and my dad planned a day at the park with Tina and River. I'm regretting not joining them." Sunny sighed, rubbing her temples.

Ma tossed a scarf around Granny Gert's neck while Chloe lectured Great Grandma Tootsie on the dangers of horizontal stripes after seventy. Gert snatched the scarf off and threw it onto the purse rack, setting off a chain reaction that sent four handbags tumbling to the floor.

"More leopard print!" Fiona announced, shuffling through a rack of summer dresses with the aggression of a professional wrestler.

"More Greek cotton!" Aunt Tasoula shouted.

"You want Greek cotton?" barked Fiona, adjusting her leather pants. "You get naked and wrap up in a bedsheet like a real goddess!"

Sunny covered a snort with a fake cough.

I closed my eyes, inhaled deeply through my nose, and tried to recenter. *They're just shopping,* I told myself. *Just shopping.* But when I opened my eyes again, I saw it—the sneaky glances. The way Chloe sidled up to the candles. How Ma poked at the drawer behind the counter. Aunt Tasoula lifting the lid of the storage ottoman with her foot while pretending to admire a tunic. *They're not shopping.*

They were searching.

One slow, focused breath later, I brushed against Chloe—just a little—and immediately caught the thought fluttering off her like a badly hidden memo. *Find the drive. Jaz think she smart, but we clever. Somewhere, Kalli's secret wedding plans are hidden!*

My eyes snapped open. "Seriously?" I said louder than I intended. All six women froze. The air buzzed with guilt. You could practically hear the imaginary record scratch. "You're looking for the drive, aren't you?"

Chloe sniffed. "I no know what you mean, Kalli mou."

"You think I'm hiding secret wedding plans," I said, my arms crossed.

"We think you're hiding *something*," Fiona countered, giving me a squinty stare over her rhinestone glasses.

"There's no drive!" I cried. "There never was! I simplified everything! I'm barely having centerpieces, let alone secret schematics!" I hadn't meant to shout, but they were driving me insane.

Aunt Tasoula and Ma exchanged skeptical glances.

"Weren't you supposed to be looking for a nice Greek girl for Jasper?" I tried to change the subject.

"Pfft." Ma huffed. "That boy too picky."

"You need us more," Aunt Tasoula added. "We no leave you in you time of need, Kalliope."

I groaned and barely suppressed an eyeroll.

Granny Gert leaned in and whispered loudly to Fiona, "She's hiding it in her loft. I just know it."

"We're not leaving empty-handed," Tootsie announced. "Land sakes, child. Operation Bridal Intel has just begun."

Sunny coughed so hard she had to pretend it was from eating a cookie.

Jaz leaned in and whispered, "They're giving themselves a mission name? The trio are as crazy as the mamas."

I sighed and pointed at them sternly. "Operation Cancel Your Madness, that's your *new* mission."

They just smiled like they were proud of themselves. Like this had been a bonding exercise for their new kooky crew, not a boutique invasion.

"Behave, ladies, or your shopping trip is over," Jaz said sternly, to which she was ignored.

Sunny sidled up to me while they noisily inspected a jewelry stand, their voices a low chorus of *"too gaudy,"* and *"too plain,"* and *"this would look better with a push-up bra."* "I repeat, I'm so sorry. They insisted on a shopping. ," she whispered, still chewing on a cookie. "They are uncontainable."

"You're acting weird lately, too," I said under my breath. "You sure you're okay?"

She smiled tightly. "Fine. Totally fine. Just, you know ... vibing at a high level of chaos today."

I didn't buy it for a second. She knew something. But I also knew Sunny—if she wasn't telling me yet, it was because she thought it would protect me, so I let it go ... for now.

Across the boutique, Great Grandma Tootsie was lifting up a yoga bolster like it might be hollowed out and full of state secrets.

I sighed and scrubbed my hands over my face.

At the counter, Chloe and Ma were huddled with Fiona and Granny Gert whispering, but we could literally hear every word.

"We move at dawn," Ma was saying dramatically. "First, we storm church, then we search storage closet. Ozzy let us in."

"I'll make pie for cover," Fiona offered.

"And cookies from me," Granny Gert added.

"And Tootsie create distraction," Chloe suggested. "She bring booze."

"Cheers," said Tootsie with a wink.

Aunt Tasoula grinned. "You want scene? I give Ostrich performance."

"Oscar, you nitwit," Ma snapped.

"You jealous." Aunt Tasoula fluffed her hair.

I looked at Sunny, my mouth half open in horror. "We are doomed," I whispered.

She nodded gravely, popping another gluten-free cookie into her mouth. "Very."

When they finally broke their "huddle," all looking suspiciously pleased with themselves, Chloe turned to us with a dazzling, *completely fake* innocent smile. "Girls, it been lovely. Such beautiful shop. So much ambiance." She strolled dramatically toward the door.

"My word, so many secrets," Granny Gert added under her breath.

"Have a *blessed day!*" Fiona chirped, winking broadly.

They sailed out the door in a cloud of strong perfume and questionable intentions, their sandals slapping determinedly against the sidewalk in time with Tootsie's cane. The bell chimed behind them, leaving Jaz, Sunny, and me standing there in the stunned, glittery aftermath.

Jaz picked up the abandoned Tupperware of cookies and shook her head. "How much time do we have before they start tunneling under the church?"

Sunny wiped her face with a napkin and sighed. "At this point, maybe we should just give them a fake drive hidden inside a Bible and call it a day."

I noticed a piece of paper with red writing on it on the floor by the door. It must have fallen out of one of their massive handbags. Picking it up, I read:

Operation Bridal Intel:

Protect the Plans, Preserve the Honor, and Prevent Catastrophe at All Costs

Code Names:

- **Ophelia (self-appointed mission leader): Agent Kalamata**
- (Briny, bold, and impossible to ignore!)
- **Tasoula (mission strategist): Agent Loukoumades**
- (Looks sweet. Will absolutely take you down.)
- **Chloe: Agent Evil Eye**
- (Warding off bad luck ... and causing a little.)
- **Granny Gert: Agent Baklava**
- (Sweet but deadly—and sticks to everything!)
- **Fiona: Agent Spanakopita**
- (Flaky on the outside, scheming on the inside!)
- **Great Grandma Tootsie: Agent Ouzo**
- (One sip and you'll never know what hit you!)

Official Rules:

Rule #1: Trust no one under sixty.
(Young people are slippery. Especially brides.)
Rule #2: If questioned, blame the moussaka.
(Preferably one made by a rival Greek mama.)
Rule #3: Spanakopita is acceptable bribe currency.
(Deploy carefully. Save baklava for emergencies.)
Rule #4: Should cover be blown, fake a sprained ankle or heart palpitations.
(Theatrics mandatory.)

Rule #5: If caught red-handed, compliment the victim's hair and change the subject immediately.
(Works 92% of the time.)
Rule #6: Never leave an ouzo flask behind.
(Evidence disposal is critical.)
Rule #7: Codename usage is mandatory in public settings.
(Example: "Agent Baklava, initiate distraction pattern!")
Rule #8: No mission is complete without snacks.
(Hangry agents compromise security.)
Rule #9: Assume the drive is hidden everywhere.
(Including but not limited to flowerpots, diaper bags, and hair buns.)
Rule #10: The bride will lie. It is your sacred duty to uncover the truth—for her own good, of course.

Mission Motto:
"Where there's a will, there's a Greek mama with a purse full of pastry and questions you don't want to answer."

Disclaimer:
The previous content is a direct transcription (or summary) of material created by a band of geriatric lunatics. It is provided solely for information purposes. The views, opinions, statements, or actions expressed within do not reflect my own and are not endorsed by me. I am not the creator of the original material and do not assume any responsibility or liability for its content accuracy, or any consequences resulting from its use. I simply had the only legible handwriting.

Respectfully,
Vivian Meadows

I watched them disappear down the street like a tactical unit disguised as a senior citizen book club and muttered, "Clearview never stood a chance."

Sunny

Later that afternoon I stepped outside of *Clearview Hotel's* bright welcoming lobby, ready to run errands with Mitch, when a cold rush of something darker slammed into me. I stumbled a little, my hand pressed to my forehead. The ground seemed to tilt under my feet. And then the vision came.

An alleyway.

Boomer, hunched and bleeding, trying to shield his ribs.

Shadows looming over him—men in dark suits, fists like hammers.

Hissed words, "Drive. Where is it?"

A boot connecting hard with Boomer's side.

A glint of something silver.

And Boomer's voice, raw and broken: "You're too late."

I gasped and blinked back into reality, my heart racing so fast it hurt.

"Sunny?" Mitch's voice snapped me into focus. He was leaning against our SUV, sipping his travel coffee while he waited for me.

I ran to him. "It's Boomer," I blurted. "He's in trouble. Bad trouble."

Mitch's smile vanished. "Vision?"

I nodded, already reaching for my phone. "I saw him getting jumped in an alley. They're beating him. They're demanding the drive."

Mitch grabbed his phone from his pocket and immediately called Nik.

It rang once before Nik answered. His voice was sharp and urgent. "Mitch?"

"Where's Boomer?" Mitch asked. "Sunny had a vision. He's hurt."

There was a pause—then a sharp intake of breath. "We've been trying to reach him for the last hour. No answer."

"We're on it," Mitch said, already pulling open the car door. "Where do we start?"

Nik rattled off a few spots Boomer was supposed to be checking—places on the outskirts of town where Ferraro's men had been spotted earlier that week.

"We'll find him," Mitch promised grimly, and we took off.

We hit every spot on Nik's list—an abandoned strip mall, the warehouse district, even the old train depot. Nothing. Then, as we were driving along a narrow industrial road lined with broken streetlights and dumpsters, I felt it again—that pull. That heavy, cold anchor in my chest that always came with a vision close to coming true.

"Stop!" I cried, slapping my hand against the dashboard.

Mitch hit the brakes, tires crunching gravel, and threw the car into park. I was already out, running toward the mouth of an alley between two warehouses, ignoring the sting of pebbles digging into my sandals.

And there he was. Boomer, slumped against the brick wall, barely conscious. Blood smeared his temple. His shirt was torn, one arm cradling his ribs.

"Boomer!" I shouted.

He lifted his head weakly, one eye already swelling shut.

Mitch was right behind me, dropping to his knees

and checking Boomer's pulse. "Stay with us, buddy. Hang in there."

Boomer tried to speak but coughed instead, his face contorting in pain.

Mitch barked into his radio for an ambulance, giving the coordinates. Within minutes, flashing lights lit up the alley. Nik arrived just as the EMTs were loading Boomer onto a stretcher. His face was pale with rage and worry.

"I'm riding with him," Nik said, climbing into the ambulance without hesitation and they took off in seconds.

Mitch and I headed to the hospital but were behind a ways, the lights of town blurring past as my heart twisted painfully in my chest. We finally reached the hospital, parked, and ran inside. The hospital waiting room was an odd combination of sterile white walls and scuffed linoleum floors, the scent of antiseptic hanging thickly in the air.

Captain Crenshaw and Mayor Zimmerman were already there when we arrived, both grim-faced and whispering in low, urgent tones. Nik must have called them from the ambulance. Captain spotted us first and waved us over.

"Status?" Mitch asked.

Captain shook his head. "He's alive. Barely. In surgery now."

"Ferraro's men," Nik said as he stepped through the ER doors, his voice low but carrying enough weight to freeze the room.

The mayor exchanged a look with the captain, then asked Nik, "Boomer confirmed this?"

Nik nodded. "They were trying to find the drive. They think Boomer has it."

"Does he?" the mayor asked sharply.

Nik shook his head. "Only the fake one."

I could see the captain doing mental math behind his steely gaze. "Meaning?"

"Meaning Boomer was bait," Nik said flatly. "Trying to draw them out. He was supposed to wait for backup, but he went rogue."

The mayor scrubbed a hand over her face. "This was handled poorly, Detective."

At that moment, the door to the ER swung open again—and Kalli and Jaz came charging in. They had that wild, focused look that meant they'd overheard *just enough* to be furious.

"You knew?" Kalli demanded, her voice shaking.

Nik paled. "Ballas—"

"You knew Ferraro's men were sniffing around," she said, stepping closer. "You knew Boomer was at risk. That the mamas could be at risk."

Jaz crossed her arms. "You let us run around town playing clueless while you dangled fake bait with my husband?"

My heart clenched. I hated seeing Kalli hurt.

Nik held his hands up, trying to calm them. "We didn't want to worry you—"

"You mean *lie* to us," Jaz snapped.

Kalli's eyes glittered with betrayal. "You should've told us. We're not porcelain dolls."

Mitch moved to step in, but Kalli held up a hand. "No. Let him answer."

Nik sighed, raking his hand through his hair. He looked ten years older in that moment. "We wanted to protect you. And the mamas. This is police business. It wasn't supposed to get this far."

"Well," Jaz said, her voice ice-cold, "guess what? It *has*."

There was a long silence, heavy and painful.

"I'm sorry," Nik said finally.

"We all are," Mitch added quietly.

I looked at Kalli's face—the mix of fury and heart-break—and my heart cracked a little too. This wasn't just about secrets. It was about trust.

And we had broken hers.

16

KALLI

Later that evening, we all sat in stiff plastic chairs under the harsh fluorescent lights of the hospital waiting room, waiting for news. The vending machines buzzed. The clock ticked too loudly. The world outside kept spinning while we sat in limbo.

I watched Sunny out of the corner of my eye, her hands clenched in her lap, and Jaz was pacing like a caged tiger. I was still so angry they had all kept Jaz and me in the dark. We weren't cops, and telling too many people *could* compromise the mission. I get that. But still, we had helped solve cases before. Yes, planning a wedding was stressful, but we were supposed to be a team. Not telling us put both of us, as well as the mamas and even the trio, in danger.

The surgeon finally came out and told us Boomer was still in surgery, but stable and in for a long recovery. He would keep us informed.

Nik stood and crossed the waiting room to me. He didn't say anything. Just pulled me into his arms and held me. I resisted for half a second before melting against him, burying my face in his chest and crying.

I'm so sorry, my love. I really was just trying to protect you and Jaz both. Please forgive me.

I didn't say anything; I didn't trust myself to say something I might regret, so I just hugged him tighter. It was all I could offer him right now.

Jaz wiped at her eyes angrily. "I still don't forgive you."

Nik smiled sadly. "I understand, but I hope you will some day."

But we all knew—this wasn't over. Ferraro's men were still out there. The real drive was still missing. And the wedding? That could possibly be the biggest casualty of all. I was hurt. My trust had been broken. And I honestly didn't know what I wanted to do about it. Not to mention, I still hadn't heard from my birth father. I'd checked in with his church. They said communication was always spotty on sabbatical. That didn't stop me from worrying. Now that he was back in my life, I couldn't imagine having my wedding without him there. Everything was such a mess.

It had been quiet for almost half an hour. Too quiet.

I sat curled up next to Nik, still silent but calmer, trying to work out the thoughts running through my head. Jaz had finally stopped pacing and was now raiding the vending machine, muttering about emotional support candy. I was just about to suggest a coffee run when the automatic doors to the ER waiting room *whooshed* open like the entrance to a bad soap opera.

And in marched Chloe, Ophelia, and Aunt Tasoula, in full battle regalia: Sunglasses so large they could double as riot shields, matching leather handbags the size of tactical backpacks, and expressions of pure, lethal determination.

Behind them, like backup called in from an under-cover operation, came Granny Gert, Fiona, and Great Grandma Tootsie, each looking ready to topple Mount Olympus or at least tackle a thug.

"What happen?" Chloe barked, planting herself in front of Nik like a Greek avenging angel.

"Where the enemy?" Aunt Tasoula demanded, cracking her knuckles.

"Which kneecaps need smashing?" Ma added, pulling Tootsie's metal travel cane from her purse like she meant to joust someone.

I groaned softly and dropped my forehead into my hands. "Oh no. Who blew the conch to Mount Olympus?"

"The mamas have *sources*," Fiona said, tapping her fingernails on her bag. "And *ears* everywhere."

"I read the police scanner," Tootsie said, pulling out a transistor radio from her purse like it was 1952. "Never leave home without it or my cane."

"I carry cookies as bribes, don't you know." Granny Gert patted her bag and then tightened her apron.

Nik rose slowly, his hands out in front of him like he was calming down a mob on a mission. "Everyone is okay," he said carefully. "Well. Boomer's not okay—but he's alive."

"Boomer like one of our babies," Chloe said, her voice low and deadly. "That a big no no."

Sunny whispered to Mitch, "Do you think they're packing rolling pins?"

Mitch grunted. "I'd be more worried about the Tupperware. It's reinforced."

Aunt Tasoula pointed dramatically toward the hospital hallway. "We demand justice!"

"We scare bad guys straight." Ophelia nodded, her

beehive swaying as she slapped the cane over and over in her hand.

Nik pinched the bridge of his nose. "Ladies. We have professionals handling this."

"Pfft," Great Grandma Tootsie snorted. "Sound like amateurs, if you ask me. I can still dance around the truth better than half the men on the police force, I wager. Can spot a liar a mile away, too."

"And my cookies are like truth serum," Granny Gert declared.

"And I can charm out the rest of the information," Fiona said with a sly wink that made the captain, lurking awkwardly in the corner, choke on his coffee.

Mitch arched a brow, studying the six of them. "At this rate, we should just swear them in."

Sunny crossed her arms and looked at the mamas and the trio. "Are you planning to storm the ICU?"

Chloe pulled a very official-looking clipboard from her bag and said crisply, "*Phase One: Information Extraction. Phase Two: Locate bad guys. Phase Three: Protect our babies at all Costs.*"

Oh my, Zeus! How many missions did they have?

Boomer's surgeon chose that moment to walk past the waiting room. He stopped mid-step, taking in the new additions to our crowd. "You here for Mr. Matheson as well?" he asked, looking vaguely terrified.

Ma turned, her eyes flashing as she patted her ample bosom. "We his family."

The surgeon wisely decided not to argue and gave a quick update about Boomer being out of surgery and finally in recovery, and that it would still be a while before he could have visitors. Once he retreated —quickly—the mamas and trio regrouped in a huddle, strategizing.

I caught snippets:

"... distract security with cookies."

"... fake fainting spells if necessary."

"... if all else fails, flash an ankle."

Jaz, sitting cross-legged on a plastic chair, murmured, "What is happening?"

She just sat there, eyes wide, as Aunt Tasoula marched up and handed her a miniature bottle of holy water from her purse. "Protection." She made the sign of the cross.

"And spanakopita for strength," Ma added, plunking down a foil-wrapped triangle of pastry in Jaz's lap.

"And a flask of courage." Tootsie winked, tucking a small silver flask into Jaz's purse.

By the time they were done, Jaz looked like she'd been anointed for battle.

"Feel better?" Ma asked me softly.

"Oddly, yes." I blinked, realizing it was true. My family might be a bit eccentric, but they were always there for me.

"Good," Chloe said, clapping her hands. "Now, sit tight. We handle from here."

And they swept out of the waiting room as dramatically as they'd arrived, leaving a trail of perfume, pastry crumbs, and pure chaos in their wake.

Mitch looked at Nik and said, "You know they're already halfway to planning a heist, right?"

Nik just nodded, looking exhausted. "I'm just hoping they don't steal an ambulance for their getaway vehicle. Might be time to put a security detail on them."

"Good idea." Mitch shook his head.

I leaned my head on Nik's shoulder, laughing quietly. The mamas were on the warpath. Boomer was alive, and somewhere out there ... Ferraro's men were about to find out the hard way: In Clearview, you don't mess with family.

Especially not when they come equipped with baklava and brass knuckles.

WE WERE HALFWAY through sharing a cold cup of waiting room coffee when Mitch came back, rubbing his temples like he'd just defused a bomb with nothing but a paperclip and regret. Nik trailed behind him, muttering something about "never underestimating a Greek woman with a clipboard."

I raised a brow. "So ... should I even ask?"

Nik sat down with a sigh so deep it shook the vending machine. "Let's just say Phase Two of their master plan almost became a felony."

Sunny leaned forward. "What happened?"

Mitch gave her a long look. "You know that clipboard Chloe pulled out like it was the Ten Commandments?"

Sunny nodded, intrigued. "What was it?"

"Color-coded blueprints of the ICU. Highlighted escape routes. Timed distraction windows. A decoy patient alias form filled out in Tasoula's handwriting —and a forged nurse's badge made out of laminated bingo cards."

I blinked. "Wait ... they were going to *infiltrate* the ICU?"

"Oh, it gets better," Nik said, rubbing his eyes. "Ophelia faked a fainting spell to draw attention. Granny Gert pretended to be her nurse. They had Fiona posing as an EMT student. Fiona! In heels!"

Sunny gasped. "What about the cookies?"

Mitch deadpanned, "Weaponized. They used them to bribe the front desk attendant, who gave them exactly thirty seconds before paging security. Fortunately, Nik and I intercepted them at the elevator before anyone got tackled."

"They were two minutes away from convincing a janitor to 'accidentally' wheel them in with the laundry cart," Nik added. "And I'm pretty sure Tootsie was in the process of picking a supply closet lock."

I covered my face with both hands. "Why does this feel like an Ocean's Six nobody asked for?"

Sunny snorted. "Ocean's Yiayia."

Mitch chuckled. "Tasoula told the security guard she was 'on a mission from Zeus.' We had to promise them supervised visitation and one *official* role each in the recovery vigil rotation to get them to stand down."

"And Ophelia's now in charge of 'diversion snacks,'" Nik said, motioning to the overflowing snack table by the wall. "Which means we're all gaining five pounds before Boomer wakes up."

Sunny sighed dreamily. "I love them so much."

I nodded. "Terrifying and unstoppable, but full of heart."

"Yeah," Mitch muttered. "Like a bake sale with olive oil and attitude."

Nik leaned back, closing his eyes. "I need a nap. Or possibly witness protection."

We both smiled, glancing toward the hallway where the Mamas and Trio had last disappeared, still whispering in Greek and plotting the next phase of Operation Overkill.

Family meant chaos—but also comfort.

And in Clearview, you never faced either alone.

Sunny

The world was barely awake yet.

The air smelled faintly of dew and brewed coffee from the few cafés prepping for the morning rush. Main Street was hushed and sleepy, bathed in soft gold from the rising sun. Shop lights flickered on one by one, like sleepy eyes blinking open.

I walked alongside Kalli, clutching my to-go cup of chamomile tea like a lifeline. She had her herbal blend, both hands wrapped around it, her steps brisk but her shoulders tense.

We hadn't really talked since everything exploded at the hospital. Since the truth had come out.

Since I had let her down.

Kalli sipped her tea, her silence weightier than any lecture she could have given.

I took a breath, stealing myself. "I'm sorry."

She didn't look at me, but her fingers tightened around her cup.

"I should've told you," I continued quietly. "I *wanted* to. Mitch and I both did."

Kalli finally glanced at me, her expression shuttered. "Then why didn't you?"

I kicked a pebble down the sidewalk, guilt gnawing at my insides. "Boomer insisted. He said the less you and Jaz knew, the safer you'd be. Nik backed him up."

"And you agreed?" she asked, her voice sharp.

"No," I admitted. "We didn't like it. At all. But they were scared you'd call off the wedding if you knew Ferraro's men were in town."

Kalli made a small, bitter sound. "Maybe I would've."

I didn't argue. She deserved the truth. "They thought they were protecting you," I said. "But it felt wrong not to tell you. I hated keeping it from you."

She walked in silence for another block, the soles of our shoes scuffing softly against the sidewalk. A delivery truck rumbled by, the scent of bakery bread trailing behind it.

"I get it," she said finally, her voice tight. "You were stuck between a rock and a hard place."

I turned to face her, stopping us in front of the old bookstore that wasn't even open yet. "It still wasn't right. And I'm truly sorry. From now on—no secrets. Not ever. You deserve better."

Kalli looked at me for a long moment, and finally, her shoulders sagged. "I'm still mad," she said. "But ... I know you were trying to do the right thing."

Relief washed through me, and I managed a shaky smile. "Good. Because I was about ten seconds away from bribing you with Granny Gert's cookies."

She snorted, some of the tension easing. "Bribery might still be necessary. I want the organic date ones."

"Done," I said solemnly.

We turned to head back toward Jaz's boutique so Kalli could get to work, still sipping our tea, the world slowly coming alive around us. That was when we heard it. Low voices. Heated. Angry.

I froze. Kalli's hand automatically found my wrist.

The sounds were coming from a narrow alley ahead, near the back of Damon's studio.

We ducked behind a dumpster, peeking around carefully. And there they were. Marcus, and two of his thugs, towering over Troy, who looked cornered and miserable, his back almost pressed to the crumbling brick wall.

"I told you to keep your mouth shut," Marcus growled, jabbing a finger into Troy's chest.

"I didn't have a choice!" Troy snapped, his voice cracking. "They were already suspicious! They were asking about the knife—I own a switchblade, for God's sake! They would've pegged me if I didn't give them something."

"Something?" Marcus sneered. "You gave them *me*."

Kalli tensed beside me, her knuckles white around her teacup.

"They know you sent your guys after Damon," Troy said, his voice lower now, desperate. "They know about the knives."

"Yeah, thanks to *you*," Marcus snarled.

"It's okay now. I heard the murder weapon was scissors," Troy blurted.

Marcus stepped in closer. "Forget about that, you little weasel. I need that evidence Damon had on me."

Troy's face paled. "I don't know where it is."

"You're lying," Marcus said, his voice like gravel. "I want to search your office."

"You can't—" Troy started, but Marcus grabbed his shirt and yanked him forward.

"You think I care about rules?" Marcus hissed. "If you know where Damon stashed it, you better spill now. Or next time, it won't just be a shakedown."

Troy looked genuinely terrified now, his eyes darting frantically. "I swear, I don't have it!" he stammered. "I don't know where it is!"

Marcus's grip tightened. "You're lying," he said again, his tone low and dangerous.

"I'm not," Troy pleaded, coming unhinged. "You're

not the only one who's done something illegal that Damon was threatening!"

Kalli and I exchanged a quick, wide-eyed look.

Marcus turned, predator-sharp. "What did you say?"

Troy faltered, realizing he'd said too much. His eyes darted left and right, as if looking for a way out that wasn't there. "I didn't mean—" he started.

Marcus closed the distance between them again, towering over him. "Talk. Now."

Troy shook his head frantically. "It's none of your business."

Marcus laughed—a short, humorless sound. "I decide what's my business."

Troy lifted his chin, but his voice was thin. "I have confidential information in my office. If it gets out, I'll be ruined. You don't have a right to it."

Marcus narrowed his eyes. "What are you hiding, Troy?"

Troy's mouth twisted, like the words wanted to come out but he forced them back.

"You really want to push me today?" Marcus growled. "After you already ran your mouth?"

Troy backed up another step, hitting the wall behind him.

"Maybe I should let my friends here convince you," Marcus said, motioning to his thugs.

One of them cracked his knuckles.

The other smirked and shifted his weight like he was gearing up for a beatdown.

I felt Kalli tense beside me, saw the spark of outrage flash across her face. She met my eyes. No words needed. *Now.* We stepped out from the alleyway at the same time.

"That's enough!" Kalli called, her voice steady and

firm, cutting through the growing violence like a blade.

Marcus's head snapped up, his dark eyes narrowing as he recognized us.

"We saw everything," I said, stepping beside Kalli, ignoring the way my heart hammered in my chest as I pulled out my phone and waved it in front of me.

Marcus sneered but lifted his hands, mockingly stepping back. "You should mind your own business," he said.

"You should mind yours," Kalli shot back, not missing a beat.

For a moment, it was a standoff—two women facing down a sleazy businessman and his muscle. The early morning bustle of Main Street seemed like a world away. Here, it was just raw tension and the pulse of adrenaline.

Finally, Marcus smiled tightly and turned back to Troy. "This isn't over," he promised, his voice like a cold razor blade. "Not by a long shot." He jerked his chin at his men, and they melted into the street, disappearing into the growing flow of early risers and delivery vans as if they'd never been there at all.

Troy sagged against the wall, sweat trickling down his temple. "Thanks," he gasped. "I mean it. I—I didn't know what they were gonna do."

"Go inside," Kalli said gently. "Lock the door."

He nodded rapidly, fumbling for his keys. He darted across the alley to the side entrance of his office building, disappearing inside and twisting the deadbolt behind him with a loud *click*.

We stood there for a long second, the alley suddenly eerily quiet again.

Kalli turned to me, her face grim. "We need to get into that office."

I nodded slowly. "Whatever Troy's hiding ... it's connected to Damon." The pieces were all there—we just hadn't fit them together yet. But we were getting close. And this time, I wasn't waiting around for more blood to be spilled.

17

KALLI

Sunny and I slipped back onto the main sidewalk, blending into the foot traffic like nothing had happened, but our minds were racing. Troy had secrets. Troy had evidence. And judging by the guilt plastered across his face and the terror vibrating off him, he knew exactly why Marcus was so desperate to get his hands on it.

Maybe it wasn't just Marcus's illegal zoning deals Damon had uncovered. Maybe Damon had found dirt on more people—Troy included. And if that evidence was stashed in Troy's office, hidden somewhere between paper files and dusty records ... we had to find it before someone else did.

As we reached the edge of the street, I pulled out my phone.

Meet me at Full Disclosure at lunchtime. Emergency. Bring backup.

I hit send—to Jaz, of course—and tucked the phone back into my purse without breaking stride. She was at the hospital with Boomer but had already planned to meet me for lunch to take her mind off his long road to recovery.

What I had in mind would definitely distract her.

"We need to be smart," I said to Sunny. "If we spook Troy too much, he'll bolt. If Marcus catches him again—"

"He won't," Sunny said fiercely.

The sun glinted off the rooftops, the sky warming into that brilliant blue that promised a beautiful day. But beneath it all, in the cracks of Clearview's quaint cobblestone charm, the real battle was building. And this time?

We were ready.

BY THE TIME Jaz screeched her little black Jeep into the parking lot behind *Full Disclosure*, I had already opened the boutique and called a couple employees in to cover our shifts. Sunny had gone back to the hotel to make arrangements for the kids. Jaz hopped out, arms full like a chaotic food courier—two iced coffees, three iced teas, a bag that smelled suspiciously like heaven (aka gyros from *Diner Delights*), and her purse clamped under her elbow.

"Sorry," she said breathlessly, juggling everything onto a bench. "Traffic. Also, Kosmos gave me extra tzatziki because he said I looked stressed."

"*We* are stressed," I said, grabbing an iced tea like it was a life preserver.

"And now," she added with a mischievous grin, "we're caffeinated, fed, and ready for anything. Ocean's 5, baby."

I laughed despite myself, tension easing just a hair.

She flopped onto the bench and unwrapped a gyro, tearing into it with all the grace of a starving goat. "So. What's the plan, Danny O?"

I filled her in on what had happened this morning. Before she could close her slack jaw, Sunny came jogging up the sidewalk, waving. She wasn't alone—Jo and Zoe were with her, both carrying suspiciously oversized tote bags. Sunny plopped down beside me, her cheeks flushed from the run.

"Sorry. We had to detour—Great Grandma Tootsie wanted to know if she should stage a fake bake sale in front of Troy's office as a distraction. Granny Gert and Fiona were totally on board, of course."

Zoe rolled her eyes. "We told them no before they called the mamas. They didn't listen, of course, until we stuck the babies in front of their faces. That will hold them off for a while."

Jo set her bag down with a heavy thud. "Also, I may or may not have grabbed a toolkit from Cole's truck."

I blinked at her. "You what?"

Jo grinned. "For emergencies."

Jaz beamed. "Now *this* is a team."

We ate quickly, perched on the bench like we were planning a bank heist instead of trying to sneak a peek at a shady photographer's filing cabinet. The plan, of course, was simple.

Step One:

Casually stroll past Troy's office like we were just doing a little lunchtime window shopping.

Step Two:

Distract Troy if he was there—Sunny was nominated for this because she could talk a crow into giving up its nest.

Step Three:

Slip into the back room and find whatever Damon was hiding—and whatever Marcus was willing to kill for.

Simple ... in theory.

I wiped my hands on a napkin and crumpled it into my gyro wrapper. "Alright, ladies. You ready?"

"Born ready," Jaz said.

"I wore my get away shoes," Jo added, flexing her sneakers.

Zoe dug a pair of latex gloves out of her tote bag. "What? New mom. Always prepared."

Sunny just smiled, eyes glinting with nerves and determination. "Let's do it."

We walked down the street like five totally normal women on a totally normal lunch break, iced drinks in hand, laughing a little too loudly.

Troy's office—aka Damon's old office—didn't look like much. Plain brick, one glass door, with a tiny "Closed for Lunch" sign hanging crookedly as I'd expected. Hence the lunchtime rendezvous. The blinds were half-drawn, but I could see a light on inside.

"He's in there," Sunny whispered out of the corner of her mouth.

"Showtime," Jaz murmured.

Sunny sauntered ahead, knocking lightly on the door, peeking through the window like a nosy neighbor. We followed a few paces behind, pretending to inspect the window display at the antique shop next door. Zoe picked up an ugly ceramic rooster from the display on the sidewalk out front and cradled it like it was a priceless artifact. Jo feigned interest in a cracked glass vase.

I kept one eye on Sunny and one on the door.

Troy opened it, looking sweaty and panicked.

Sunny gave him her most disarming, friendly smile. "Hey, Troy! I was just walking by and thought I would check in, given what happened this morning. You okay?"

He looked like he wanted to slam the door and crawl under a rock. "I'm fine," he mumbled. "Busy."

Sunny tilted her head, all sweet concern. "Busy doing what? You know, if you need help organizing, I'm really good at that. I color-code *everything*."

Troy blinked. "I—I'm good."

"Are you sure?" Sunny pressed. "I could help you sort files. Give you a reading if you'd like. Maybe help you feel a little less ... overwhelmed?"

Troy's mouth opened and closed like a fish.

Perfect.

While Sunny distracted him, Jaz gave me a tiny nod. We slipped around the side of the building, where a narrow alley ran between the antique store and Troy's office. There was a side entrance—a battered blue door with a rusted lock.

Jo pulled the toolkit out of her bag like she was unwrapping a Christmas present.

"You know how to pick a lock?" I whispered, stunned.

"My ex was a locksmith," she said with a shrug. "I learned by osmosis."

Jaz and I shielded her with our bodies, pretending to dig through our purses in case anyone glanced down the alley. Jaz worked quickly, her fingers deft and confident. There was a soft *click*. The door creaked open.

We slipped inside, our hearts pounding, into a cluttered back room that smelled like dust and industrial cleaner. Stacks of old invoices, broken office chairs, toolboxes, and a defunct mini-fridge filled the space. A small hallway led toward the front of the building, where we could hear Sunny chatting animatedly about artisanal coffee beans and essential oils.

"Fast," Jaz whispered.

We split up—Jo scanning the shelves, Zoe flipping through filing cabinets, me rifling through the drawers of Troy's battered metal desk. Most of it was junk—warranties, repair invoices, unpaid bills.

But then I found it.

In the bottom drawer, under a fake-bottom panel. A thumb drive. It was labeled with a tiny piece of masking tape: **D. - OFFICIAL DOCS.** I held it up, my heart hammering so loud I thought for sure they could hear it outside.

"Got it," I whispered, stuffing it into my bag.

The front door chimed—the jingle of Troy's panicked attempt to shoo Sunny away.

"Move!" Jaz hissed.

We slipped back out the side door, Jo re-locking it with a flourish that would've made any cat burglar proud. We sprinted down the alley and then the street until we reached *Sinfully Delicious*, collapsing into a booth, breathless and giddy.

Sunny joined us thirty seconds later, laughing as she slid into the booth. "Please tell me you got something," she said.

I opened my hand, revealing the thumb drive.

Sunny's face lit up. "Kalli, you legend."

Jaz fist-bumped me under the table. *Best distraction ever.*

I smiled as Jo ordered a round of iced coffees and teas for victory. Zoe ordered pastries for all. We sat there, sipping, eating, and grinning, the adrenaline still buzzing through us.

We had it. Whatever Damon had on people—whatever Marcus was willing to threaten and possibly kill for—it was now in our hands. A look passed between Sunny and me, and I didn't have to read her mind to know we were both on the same page.

No more secrets.

Sunny

It was almost two when Zoe and Jo hugged us goodbye outside the library.

"I have to get back to nurse the baby," Zoe said, adjusting her tote bag on her shoulder. "Sean can't help with that." She laughed.

Jo gave a dramatic sigh. "And I promised I'd go to the park with Cole and the twins after their nap. Pray for me."

We waved them off, and Jaz, after a tight hug, announced she was going back to the hospital to check on Boomer.

"You okay to do this?" Kalli asked me once it was just the two of us.

"Yep," I said, adjusting my crossbody bag and trying not to yawn. "My parents have River and Tina since Mitch is helping Nik now that Boomer's out of commission. I'm not going to waste this rare window of freedom."

We marched into the library, the scent of old books and lemon cleaner greeting us like an old friend. Kalli led the way to the back where the public computers sat in a neat row.

"Faster than trying to fire up my laptop at home. It's on its last legs," she whispered.

We huddled around a computer and logged in, popping the thumb drive we'd gotten from Troy's office into the USB slot. I clicked open the first folder, my heart hammering with a weird mixture of nerves and excitement.

The first document was a series of spreadsheets. "Oh my, Zeus," Kalli muttered. "This confirms that Marcus was bribing town officials. I just never realized how many could be bought."

"For what?" I leaned over.

"Zoning permits. Look—" She pointed at a list of names and dollar amounts. "To get his real estate projects fast-tracked. No wonder he built so fast. This information could damage his reputation for sure."

"Wow." I scrunched my face. "I don't know him that well, but somehow it doesn't surprise me." I clicked to the next folder. "Wait. There's information on Angela."

The screen filled with scanned copies of emails. My eyes widened as I scrolled. "Oh, my Lord—years ago, Angela really did spread fake rumors about the head seamstress at her old job like she admitted, I just didn't know how bad it was. It says here that she told people that the seamstress stole designs and slept with her boss. That poor woman. She ruined her, and yet none of it was true according to Damon's notes."

"And then Angela stole the woman's clients," Kalli finished, disgust dripping from her voice.

"Exactly." I stared in shock. Kalli and I were both businesswomen, yet I couldn't imagine either of us doing something like this. We said we wouldn't judge her, but it was hard not to.

"No wonder Angela is so obsessed with making it big," Kalli muttered. "She bulldozed her way up to the top." Kalli's face filled with pity. "Such a shame. She's a highly respected seamstress here in Clearview. She seems to have changed, but that doesn't excuse what she did to her boss and how desperate she acts to keep this information hidden."

I kept clicking through the drive. My stomach twisted as the next folder opened—full of photos.

"Sunny," Kalli whispered.

The pictures showed Vanessa—no mistaking that sleek auburn hair and designer stilettos—in compromising positions with a man old enough to be her father. A man I recognized from the society pages: married to a woman who donated a million dollars a year to the hospital. These were far more explicit than the pictures Ozzy found in the church storage room.

"Vanessa was sleeping with a married rich guy. A wedding she helped plan," I mused. "This would ruin her if it got out."

"How Damon got ahold of those pictures is beyond me," Kalli said grimly.

We exchanged a glance. There was a pattern here. Damon had so many enemies who had motive to want him dead.

"Wait," Kalli said. "What's this?" She clicked into another folder.

"Lila," I read. My mouth went dry. "It says she's an addict, just like I suspected from my vision at her house that day."

"And that's not all," Kalli murmured, scrolling through financial documents. "Her inheritance—her grandfather's trust fund—Damon was bleeding it dry for years before the divorce."

"No wonder she hates him." I frowned. "But ... there's more." We found texts and photos—Lila and Barry.

"They were having an affair!" Kalli blurted in a stunned voice.

"That explains Damon and Barry's falling out," I said, nodding.

"That and whatever went wrong at that event they worked together that they blamed each other for," Kalli added.

"My guess is Barry was the problem. Look." I pointed. More texts revealed Barry's drug problem—and that he'd dragged Lila down with him.

"So, she's been using?" Kalli whispered.

I nodded grimly. "He's the one who got her hooked."

"Which means Damon probably knew and used it against her in the divorce," Kalli said. "He had notes that he had an affair in retaliation. A woman in another town named Amy Davis. He played the pity card and took her for all she was worth but then broke it off when the woman grew needy and demanded more of him. He dumped her coldly and never looked back." She looked up with misty eyes. "He really was a cruel man."

I nodded sadly and then thought about the pieces we were still missing. "Vivienne must fit in here somewhere," I said, frowning at the screen. "But how?"

"And what didn't Josh want to do anymore?" Kalli asked. "There's nothing in here about him."

We filed that thought away for later and moved on.

"Last folder," Kalli said.

Troy. We knew about his gambling addiction—he hadn't exactly hidden it well. But the next file made my stomach drop.

"He owed serious money to loan sharks," I read aloud, the words making my skin prickle.

"And Damon found out," Kalli said, her voice low.

More documents detailed it clearly: Damon blackmailed Troy into robbing guests at weddings—stealing jewelry, cash, anything easy to snatch—and giving Damon a cut to keep him quiet.

"If Troy refused, Damon threatened to turn him in," Kalli said, disgusted. "Damon was the shadiest person of all, but he kept his hands clean by using people to do his dirty work and give him favors."

I leaned back in the creaky library chair, rubbing my temples. "No wonder Troy looked sick every time a wedding rolled around."

"And no wonder he was scared of Marcus," Kalli added. "If Marcus found out and Damon knew ... Troy was trapped."

We stared at each other for a long moment, the air between us heavy with everything we'd just uncovered.

"It's a blackmail network," I said finally. "Damon had half the town in his pocket."

I shut down the computer, my hands shaking slightly. I suddenly got the strangest sensation of being watched. Kalli must have felt it too because she glanced around to make sure no one had heard us, then she tucked the drive back into her bag. I didn't want to know what people would do to get their hands on this. We slipped out of the library into the cooling late afternoon.

Across the street, the streetlamps flicked on, one by one, casting pools of gold on the cracked sidewalks as early evening approached.

"You know what this means, right?" I said as we crossed the street to Kalli's car.

"That we're officially in way over our heads?" she quipped. "As much as I love our sleuthing escapades as the Mystical Mavens, I think it's time to bring our detectives in on this. Tonight. After Jaz and I close up the boutique. It's time some arrests were made and at least some of our leads get wrapped up."

"I think you're right," I said.

Then we both added simultaneously, "No more secrets."

18

KALLI

I locked the front door of *Full Disclosure* and turned the key with a satisfying click. The boutique windows reflected the last blush of sunset, but inside, the racks of boho dresses and handmade jewelry already looked ghostly in the dim light.

"That's it," I said, turning to Jaz, who stood behind the register counting down the drawer. "Another day, another small fortune in credit card receipts."

Jaz chuckled and shoved the till closed. "Small fortune is right. I sold four scarves and a pair of jeans. You sold several pieces of lingerie. Big spender energy."

I laughed, but it felt forced. My nerves were still buzzing from everything Sunny and I had uncovered earlier. I couldn't stop thinking about the flash drive burning a hole in my purse. "So, how's Boomer doing?" We'd been too busy to catch up since Jaz had visited him last.

"Better," Jaz said as we headed toward the back room. She kept her voice casual, but I caught the tightness in it. "He's pretty banged up and in pain, but he wants out. Wants real food, not hospital slop."

Relief bloomed through my chest. "Sounds just

like how Nik and Mitch would be. Too stubborn not to pull through."

"Yeah," she said, but her smile faltered. "Still ... he's got a long road."

We reached the back door, and I hesitated. I needed to tell her before I chickened out. "Jaz, wait," I said, pulling the flash drive from my bag and holding it between two fingers. "Sunny and I looked at this in the library earlier."

Her brow furrowed. "What was on it?"

"Everything," I said, my voice barely a whisper. "Marcus bribing town officials. Angela stealing clients and ruining reputations. Vanessa cheating with married country club clients. And get this—Barry and Lila? They were having an affair. Barry's the one who got Lila hooked on drugs."

Jaz's mouth dropped open. "You're kidding me."

"I wish. And it gets worse. Troy's the one robbing weddings. Damon caught him owing money to loan sharks for his gambling addiction and blackmailed him into stealing for him."

Her hands flew to her mouth. "Troy?"

"I know," I said. "I'm giving the drive to Nik tonight. As soon as he gets home."

We exchanged a look, heavy with understanding. This could finally be the break we needed to blow everything open—end Marcus, Damon, and every last rotten game they played with our town. And hopefully find a murderer in our midst.

Jaz reached for the lock, flipping it open. "Come on. Let's get outta here. I don't like you having all that power in your bag. Too many people would kill to get their hands on it."

"Oh, trust me, I'm more than ready to hand it over to the authorities."

The parking lot behind the shop was empty, the lamplight buzzing weakly overhead. My heels clicked against the asphalt as we made our way toward our cars. I fished for my keys, balancing the flash drive like a talisman in my palm.

That's when I heard it.

The faint scrape of a shoe. Before I could even turn, arms clamped around me, pinning my arms to my sides. My purse hit the ground with a dull thud. *Fight harder. I like it.* I swallowed hard and tried to block out his thoughts.

"Kalli!" Jaz screamed, but her voice was cut off, muffled. She was being grabbed too.

"Hey! Let us—" I tried to kick, bite, anything, but a rough cloth pressed against my mouth, cutting off my words. My heart hammered wildly against my ribs. I fought harder, but it was useless. They were too strong.

Blindfolds were tied over our eyes. I felt myself being shoved forward, my feet stumbling over cracked asphalt, dragged like a rag doll. The contact was too fleeting to pick up any more thoughts, but I had a feeling it was Marcus's men. After standing up to him this morning, I doubted he would let it go that easily.

We were stuffed into the back of a van, the door slamming shut behind us. The vehicle rumbled to life, the hum of tires on back roads growing louder as we picked up speed.

I tried to track the turns. Left. Right. Another right. I didn't recognize the pattern, but after a while, I smelled pine needles and campfire smoke.

We were somewhere near *Clearview Park* ... farther out. A shudder ran through me. They weren't taking us to Marcus. He lived in Clearview, so he wouldn't stay in the park. This was something worse.

Finally, the van jerked to a stop. Rough hands yanked me out. *You're a feisty one. I'm going to enjoy this.* I jerked away from his touch, and my sneakers scraped dirt and gravel. We were marched several feet before a door squealed open and we were thrown inside what smelled like whiskey and stale air as it rocked.

A camper.

The blindfold was yanked off me so fast I blinked hard against the harsh fluorescent lights. Jaz was dumped beside me, struggling to sit up. She looked terrified—and furious. Then I saw him.

It had to be Dominic Ferraro from the way Nik had described him. Powerful, sharp-eyed, expensive suit, and absolutely radiating menace as he leaned against the cheap kitchen counter inside the camper. Four of his men flanked the walls, guns tucked casually into their waistbands like they were part of the decor.

"Welcome," Dominic said smoothly. "This isn't exactly my style, but it will do for what I have planned. Hope you enjoyed your non-scenic tour."

"What do you want?" I rasped. My voice cracked from the cloth gagging me earlier.

He pushed off the counter and sauntered toward us, every step deliberate. "You two made a mistake tonight."

"We don't know what you're talking about," Jaz said quickly, trying to sound braver than she probably felt.

"Oh, I think you do," he said, crouching in front of us. His cold gaze fixed on my purse lying a few feet away. "You have something that belongs to me."

I shook my head, my heart pounding. "No, we don't. It's not what you think—"

But he wasn't listening. One of his men picked up my bag and dumped it upside down. Lip gloss, receipts, hair ties—and the thumb drive—spilled onto the dirty linoleum.

Dominic picked it up, holding it between two fingers like it was radioactive. "You think I don't know who you are, Kalli Ballas?" he said, his voice silky and terrifying. "You think I didn't have eyes on you and your friend when you went poking around the library?"

And here I thought it had been Marcus.

Jaz stiffened beside me. "It's not yours," she said. "It's not even about you!"

Dominic's mouth curled with a bitter smile. "No? Looks like evidence to me. Evidence from Boomer's little undercover days when he tried to take down my operation."

My stomach twisted. He thought the drive was from *that* case. "It's not," I pleaded. "It's not from back then. It's about Marcus! It's about Damon! Several people, but not you!"

"You're lying," Dominic said softly, deadly. "And liars don't get second chances."

He turned the thumb drive over in his hand thoughtfully and then shoved it into his pocket.

"Please," Jaz said, her voice cracking now. She pushed herself up onto her knees. "Please don't hurt us. We didn't do anything to you. Let us go."

His face darkened. "I lost my Isabella because of Boomer. My sweet girl, caught in a shootout meant for him." He took a step back, nodding to his men. "You want to make him pay?" Dominic said, his voice shaking with fury. "Then you take away what he loves. That's the only reason I left him alive in that alley. So *he* would know how I felt."

The men grabbed Jaz roughly, hauling her to her feet. She screamed and kicked, but it was no use.

I lunged forward, but one of them slammed me back down with a boot against my shoulder. "Stop!" I shrieked, tears blurring my vision. "Stop, please, she didn't do anything!"

But Dominic's eyes were cold, soulless. "An eye for an eye," he said.

I fought against the weight pressing me down, but I couldn't move fast enough.

"Boomer will finally know," Dominic said, pulling out a pistol and cocking it. "He'll feel exactly what I felt." The gun leveled at Jaz's head.

"No!" I screamed, my voice tearing from my throat. "There's more evidence, and I know where it is." It was a lie, but it hopefully bought us some time.

Sunny

The phone rang and rang, but Kalli didn't answer.

I frowned, pacing the living room of our suite, my bare feet wearing a path on the carpeted floor. "Come on, Kalli, pick up."

I tried Jaz next. Same thing. Straight to voicemail.

Something prickled along my spine—a sense of wrongness I couldn't shake. I grabbed my cell tighter and called Mitch, who was still at the station finishing up paperwork. He'd headed there after I'd gotten home from the library.

"Hey, Tink," he answered, a smile in his voice. "What's up?"

"Have you heard from Nik?"

He paused. "Not since earlier. Why?"

"I can't get ahold of Kalli or Jaz. I was just going to

check in and see if Kalli gave Nik the thumb drive, but ..." I trailed off, dread pooling in my gut.

"Hang on." I heard him fumbling, then muttering. "I'm calling him now."

I waited, my stomach knotting tighter with every second. Mitch had him on speaker on the office line, and I could hear him through my cell phone.

Nik picked up on the third ring, sounding tired. "Hey, Mitch. Just got back from checking on Boomer. He's doing better."

"Good," Mitch said, then cut to the chase. "You with Kalli?"

There was a pause. A long one. "No," Nik said slowly. "She said she was locking up with Jaz tonight, and we would talk when she got home. Why?"

"Because no one's heard from either of them," Mitch said grimly. "Sunny tried. They're not answering."

I heard Nik swear under his breath. "Give me two minutes. I'm coming."

I didn't wait. I was already grabbing my purse and keys. "I'm heading to *Aphrodite's*," I said. "The mamas might know something."

Mitch cursed this time. "Sunny, wait for us. Don't do anything stupid."

"Me? Never," I said, already halfway out the door.

The restaurant was still bustling when I pushed inside. The scent of garlic and lemon filled the air, but all I could taste was fear. Ophelia, Tasoula, and Chloe were gathered around their usual table, playing cards and drinking coffee.

"Sunny, koukla!" Chloe called out. "Come, sit. You look pale. Have a cookie!"

"No time," I said, hurrying over. "Have you seen Kalli or Jaz tonight?"

All three women exchanged looks.

"No," Ophelia said slowly. "They say they closing boutique. Why?"

I didn't answer. Instead, my gaze landed on Kalli's soft gray cardigan draped over the back of a chair. She always left it here for when the restaurant's AC got too cold. I reached out and grabbed it, hoping to pick up a reading for something. Anything.

The vision slammed into me like a freight train.

Darkness. Pine trees. A camper with peeling paint. Inside—Kalli and Jaz, tied up, terrified. A man—it looked like Dominic Ferraro from Boomer's files—stood over them, a gun pointed at Jaz's head. His face twisted in rage.

I gasped and staggered back.

"Sunny!" Chloe cried, catching my elbow.

"They're in trouble," I whispered, my heart pounding so hard it hurt.

Nik and Mitch burst through the door a second later.

"Ferraro has them," I said. "They're in a camper."

Mitch's face hardened. "You're sure?"

I nodded, still trembling.

"The campground just outside of *Clearview Park* recently opened for the summer," Nik said grimly. "Plenty of places to hide out there."

Mitch turned to me with a stern look. "Sunny, you stay here. Things are too dangerous now. Think of our children." I opened my mouth to argue, but he cut me off with a look that brooked no argument. "You *stay*." Then he added as an afterthought, "Please."

Smart man.

Nik yanked out his phone and dialed. "Boomer? It's Nik. We got a situation. Ferraro's got Kalli and Jaz at *Clearview Park*."

I caught Boomer's grave reply, "I'm making a call."

Nik and Mitch didn't waste another second. They charged out the door, weapons hidden under their jackets. I stood there for maybe two heartbeats before my legs moved on their own.

There was no way I was staying behind while my best friend was in danger.

I headed to *Clearview Park* and parked off the road in a hidden spot. Somehow, I beat the guys to the park. Making my way to the campground, I crept through the trees, staying low, staying quiet. I wasn't stupid enough to get close ... just close enough to see which camper it was. Maybe I could distract them if things went bad. Maybe I could—

A hand clamped over my mouth from behind.

I struggled, but a low voice hissed, "Move and you're dead."

Dominic Ferraro's men.

If they didn't kill me, Mitch surely would.

They dragged me through the trees and shoved me inside the camper. I landed hard, scraping my knees against the floor. Kalli and Jaz both gasped.

"Sunny!" Kalli cried, trying to reach me, but the ropes around her wrists dug deep.

Dominic looked almost pleased. "Well, well. Psychic girl thought she could sneak up on us." He pulled out his gun and pointed it at my head. "I'm done playing games. Three for the price of one. I like that deal."

Outside, tires screeched against the gravel.

Nik and Mitch.

"Drop your weapons!" Nik shouted from outside. "Now!"

"We have you surrounded," Mitch added. "It's over, Ferraro. There's nowhere to run."

Ferraro's men dragged me to my feet, shoving me

in front of them like a shield as they threw open the camper door and dragged me outside.

"Drop yours," Dominic sneered, his gun aimed at my head as he stepped out beside them. "Or she dies first."

I squeezed my eyes shut. I didn't want to die. Not like this. Not here.

"Drop your gun," Mitch ground out, fury radiating from him. He was *so* not happy with me.

I opened my eyes and met his as, slowly, they both set their guns on the ground, hands raised.

Dominic's smile widened. He pressed the barrel of his gun to my temple. "Too easy," he said. "Now you're all going to know what it feels like to lose everything."

"FBI!" a voice shouted from beside Dominic, startling him.

Men in tactical gear stormed him, guns drawn.

Dominic's crew barely had time to react. Within seconds, they were disarmed, wrestled to the ground, and handcuffed. Dominic fought harder, swinging at an agent, but he was outnumbered. They pinned him fast.

I collapsed onto my knees, gasping for air.

Nik rushed forward, freeing Kalli and Jaz, checking them over frantically. "You're okay," Nik kept repeating, pulling Kalli into his arms. "You're okay, koukla. I've got you, sweetheart."

Kalli clung to him, shaking.

Mitch made sure Jaz was okay and then hauled me upright, his hands running over me as if making sure I was in one piece. "You ever scare me like that again, Sunshine, and I swear—"

"I'm okay," I whispered, tears blurring my vision. That's when I finally noticed who was standing in the doorway of the camper, staring at all of us.

Ozzy.

The quiet janitor from the Greek church, who looked like a lumberjack. Except ... far more intimidating in his tactical vest and badge.

"You're FBI?" I croaked.

Ozzy gave a sheepish grin. "Undercover. Been keeping tabs on Ferraro as soon as he slipped through our fingers and ended up in Clearview."

Nik stared at him in disbelief. "Boomer knew?"

"Boomer knew," Ozzy confirmed. "He's the one who called me when you said Ferraro grabbed them. Got the cavalry here just in time."

I sagged against Mitch in relief, the adrenaline draining out of me all at once.

We were safe ... for now.

19

KALLI

The hospital smelled like antiseptic and burnt coffee, but I was just grateful to be breathing it in. Alive. All of us were. Bruised, rattled, and emotionally shredded, sure—but alive.

Jaz sat beside me in the waiting room, her arm in a sling and a Band-Aid across her temple. Sunny paced with a cup of vending machine tea, muttering to herself and then pausing to sip, like that would somehow quiet the tremors in her hands.

It didn't.

"They're gonna call us back any second," I said, glancing at the giant clock on the wall. "They just want to make sure we're not secretly concussed or filled with internal bleeding or something cheerful like that."

Jaz snorted. "My concussion would like a croissant and a margarita."

Sunny stopped pacing. "Your concussion has excellent taste."

Eventually, a nurse called us back. A whirlwind of blood pressure cuffs, light-in-the-eye tests, and overly perky staff later, we were deemed okay. Shaken, not stirred. Just a little bruised and full of trauma. Nothing that wouldn't heal.

Physically, anyway.

But when we were finally cleared and led to Boomer's room, the pit in my stomach dropped all over again. He looked like a broken mountain lying in that bed. His usual booming laugh and ridiculous jokes had been replaced by IVs and beeping monitors. Still, he gave us a tired grin the moment we walked in.

"Look what the cat dragged in. You all look worse than me."

"Not possible," Jaz said, limping to his bedside and giving his hand a gentle squeeze.

Boomer looked at us and then beyond us. Mitch was already in the room, sitting in the corner like a watchdog in a leather jacket. Nik stood by the window, arms crossed, jaw clenched, the muscles in his forearms twitching like he was ready to punch something —or someone. Captain Crenshaw stood near the foot of the bed, not in uniform but still commanding the room like it was his precinct.

And then there was Ozzy. Our surprise undercover janitor-turned-FBI-hero, leaning against the doorframe like he'd been waiting his whole life to deliver the news he was about to drop.

"Ferraro's going away for attempted murder," Crenshaw began, his voice low and gruff.

Nik let out a humorless laugh. "That's it? After everything?"

Ozzy stepped forward. "Actually, it's not just attempted murder anymore."

We all turned toward him.

He smirked slightly. "We found the drive. The real one with everything we need. All of it."

Sunny blinked. "You mean the one we've been

chasing through bachelor parties, bribes, blackmail, and kidnappings for the last three months?"

"That's the one," Ozzy said. "Turns out Ginger Debois resurfaced."

"Ginger?" I said, stunned. "She's alive? I thought Ferraro took her out when he took out Carbone."

"She's a crafty one. Been living under the radar in Las Vegas. Changed her name. Got a job as a cocktail waitress at a piano bar." Ozzy raised an eyebrow. "She cut a deal when she heard Ferraro had slipped up and the net was tightening. Gave us the exact location of the drive in exchange for witness protection and immunity from everything."

"Where was it?" Jaz asked.

I braced myself. The answer was bound to be ridiculous.

"In the mouth of the stuffed shark," Ozzy said, deadpan.

I blinked. "I'm sorry, what?"

He chuckled. "Hanging on the wall of *The Rusty Pelican*."

"The underground poker room?" Boomer said, wincing as he tried to sit up.

"The very one," Ozzy confirmed. "Apparently Anthony 'The Shark' Carbone thought it would be funny. It's been there for years, literally staring everyone in the face."

Sunny groaned. "Hidden in plain sight. I hate criminals with a flair for the dramatic."

"Well, that drive," Ozzy continued, "has everything we need. Every wire transfer, every offshore account, names, dates, payoffs, threats, blueprints, and internal communications. It connects Ferraro to an entire network of fraud, extortion, drug trafficking, and even a judge who's now been disbarred."

Nik let out a long breath. "So, it's finally over."

Ozzy nodded. "Ferraro won't see the outside of a prison again. This time, it sticks."

Captain Crenshaw stepped forward again. "And that's not all. We've made a few more arrests since this morning."

I braced myself.

"Troy's been arrested for robbery," Crenshaw said. "Turns out Damon wasn't bluffing about the wedding heists. We have video and stolen goods in his office. Sloppy. Probably was starting to spiral."

Sunny and I exchanged a look. That Ocean's 5 mission to peek into his office hadn't been a waste after all.

"Marcus was picked up too," Crenshaw went on. "Corruption, harassment, zoning violations, tax evasion—the works. The man's going down for more than just being an insufferable jerk."

"Good," I muttered. "He's terrorized too many people for too long."

"Barry and Lila?" Jaz asked.

Crenshaw's expression tightened. "Still watching them. They're a hot mess—addicts, definitely. But no hard proof of anything criminal yet."

"Yet," Nik repeated darkly.

"And Vanessa?" Sunny asked.

"She made bad choices," Crenshaw admitted, "but sleeping with a married man isn't a crime."

Jaz tilted her head. "Morally questionable doesn't equal criminal."

"Exactly," Crenshaw said. "We'll keep an eye on her. If she gets tangled deeper into the mess, we'll know."

"And Angela?" I asked.

Now it was Mitch who spoke. "Her old boss caught

wind of the gossip. Flew back in and slapped her with a slander lawsuit. Most of her high-society clients dropped her like yesterday's tuna tartare and returned to her old boss. Fickle bunch."

"Poetic justice," Sunny said, sipping her tea again.

I looked around the room. At my bruised friends. At the man I loved silently pacing, processing everything. At the captain who had come through when it mattered. At Ozzy, who risked everything to protect a town that hadn't even known it needed protecting. And at Boomer—bruised, battered, but smiling. Still here. Still Boomer.

"We're really okay," I said softly. "Aren't we?"

Nik crossed the room and knelt in front of me, brushing a strand of hair off my cheek. "We're better than okay. We're together. We made it."

"Barely," I said.

"But we did," he repeated, and kissed my forehead.

Sunny reached over and took my hand. "Trauma-bonded for life, baby."

Jaz snorted. "We need T-shirts."

Ozzy pulled a folded piece of paper from his jacket and held it up. "Actually, what you need is this."

"What is it?" I asked.

"A formal commendation. For assisting a federal investigation and helping bring down a major criminal enterprise." He grinned. "You're all heroes. Messy, nosy, impulsive heroes—but heroes nonetheless."

I laughed. It felt foreign and raw in my chest, but real.

Boomer raised a weak fist. "To the nosiest ladies in town."

"To *The Rusty Pelican* and the shark with secrets," Sunny added.

"To getting our lives back," Jaz said.

Nik just looked at me. "To whatever comes next."

And for once, I didn't feel like running from it.

Just when I thought things were finally starting to settle, the elevator doors opened with a loud *ding*—and chaos entered.

Literally.

"I bring baklava!" Ma called out as she led the stampede down the hallway, waving a covered tin overhead like it was the Olympic torch.

"Cookies from Granny Gert!" Chloe added behind her, her arms full of baked goods and a bag of dried lavender tied with blue ribbon.

"Pie from Fiona and flask from Great Grandma Tootsie," Aunt Tasoula declared, holding up a pie case in one hand and a crystal-studded hip flask with a wink. "Doctor say fluids. He no say what *kind*. Okay? Okay."

Behind them trailed the Tasty Trio, humming, singing, and dancing into the room, smelling like honey and cinnamon and just a pinch of trouble.

Ophelia reached us first, dropping a tote bag on Boomer's bed with a thud. "Aloe and duct tape," she said triumphantly. "One soothe, one stick. Everything fix. Bodies. Emotions. Leaky faucets."

Boomer blinked. "Uh. Thank you?"

"You no worry. We patch Uncle Stratos after goat incident," she said proudly. "He good as new."

"Don't ask," Nik whispered to Boomer.

Aunt Tasoula floated in next, placing an entire spa kit on the windowsill. "Oh, woe is me." She swooned. "Our babies need self-care. Epsom salts, cucumber eye pads, and something I find on sale." She winked. "Smell like bergamot and rich divorce."

Sunny eyed it. "Honestly? It all sounds like heaven."

Chloe, wearing about three crosses and a fresh evil-eye bracelet, handed one to each of us like she was passing out anti-hex candy. "I cleanse them in holy water," she said. "And I sprinkle blessed salt in the lobby."

"I thought I heard someone sneezing in the hall," Jaz said.

"Probably," Chloe replied without remorse. "But no one curse my babies again."

"You think this was a curse?" I asked, my eyebrow arching high.

"I think someone no knock on wood for luck," Chloe said, eyeing me pointedly.

Guilty. I bit back a chuckle. "Well, thank you all."

I looked around the crowded hospital room, which now smelled like baked apples, pine resin, and the faint whiff of duct tape. Fiona, Granny Gert, and Great Grandma Tootsie were already making plans with the mamas to prepare a Greek feast when we all got home.

Sunny elbowed me gently. "You know what this means?"

"What?"

"We're going to need a bigger kitchen table."

"And possibly a restraining order for whoever said, 'things should quiet down now,'" Jaz added dryly.

Nik slung an arm around my shoulder and leaned in. "I think I like the chaos ... as long as you're in the middle of it."

"You mean duct tape and aloe chaos?" I laughed.

He kissed my temple. "Exactly that ... future Mrs. Stevens."

And for the first time in weeks, maybe even months, the thought of marrying my best friend no longer scared me.

Sunny

If someone had told me a few weeks ago that I'd be spending my Saturday at a community arts festival with a baby strapped to my chest and a paintbrush in one hand, I might've laughed—or cried. But there I was, River bouncing happily in his carrier, one sticky fist gripping a half-melted crayon, while Tina sat at a miniature picnic table, proudly gluing glitter onto what I think was supposed to be a butterfly.

The scent of kettle corn, tacos, and sunscreen wafted through *Clearview Park*. The air was filled with music from the gazebo, where Barry was the DJ, bobbing his head to a retro soul remix as he manned the booth. If the matching headband on his bald head and tinted sunglasses were meant to make him look cool, he mostly looked like someone trying a little too hard. My parents and Kalli's seemed to like it as they swayed to the music on the grassy dance area.

Jo plopped down on the bench beside me, her twin boys—Collin and Jeremiah—climbing on the jungle gym like caffeinated monkeys. "This is actually peaceful," she said, brushing Cheeto dust off her leggings.

"For now," I said, shifting River on my hip. "Let's not jinx it."

Zoe strolled up next, pushing baby Alannah in the world's largest stroller and holding two juice boxes in her mouth. She handed one to Tina and the other to Jeremiah, who took it like it was a magic elixir and disappeared into the sandbox.

I glanced over at the dog park, where Kalli, Jaz, and their pack of designer pets were gathered. Wolfgang lounged like a furry throw rug while Willow and Armani dug holes, and Versaci and Chanel chased a rogue tennis ball with synchronized grace that would've made the Rockettes proud.

Kalli waved us over, and Jo nodded. "Go. We'll stay here with the kids."

"You're brave," I said.

"I'm outnumbered either way," she shrugged. "Might as well commit."

I headed over with River and Tina in tow, not wanting to add to her pack, when Jaz intercepted us and scooped Tina up for a spin. "My favorite clever chaos machine!"

Tina giggled, squealing, "Higher, Jazzy!"

"She's a menace," I told her.

"She gets it from you," Kalli added with a smirk, passing me an iced tea from the nearby truck like a lifeline.

I took a long sip. "Bless you."

The sun glinted off the gazebo where Barry spun the next track—a breezy, synth-heavy summer jam— and nodded to the crowd like he was headlining Coachella. But something caught my eye. Near the back of the stage, Barry had stepped away and was deep in a heated conversation with his assistant, Josh.

Josh had only just graduated high school. A rough past, yes—run-ins with the law, poor grades, bad crowd. But Barry had taken him on last year, mentored him, and given him a job. Everyone said it had turned his life around. I'd even seen him helping little kids at the skate clinic and handing out bottled water at the Halloween fair.

But now his fists were clenched, his face red. Barry jabbed a finger in his chest. Josh muttered something and stormed off, his shoulders hunched and angry.

"Did you see that?" I asked.

"Yeah," Kalli said, already stepping forward.

Jaz glanced at the kids, then toward Zoe and Jo. She took River and Tina and walked over, returning shortly without them. "We'll check it out. They'll watch the gremlins. Before you say anything, Sunny, they insisted."

I nodded, and we left the music, the laughter, and the smell of hot dogs behind us as we followed Josh past the playground and into the gravel parking lot behind the food trucks. We heard it before we saw it— the unmistakable crack of metal meeting metal.

"Josh?" I called, rounding the corner.

He didn't hear—or didn't care. He raised a wooden baseball bat high and brought it down on the hood of Barry's green Lexus with a roar. Glass shattered. Metal caved.

"Whoa, stop!" Jaz yelled, racing forward.

Josh stumbled back, dropping the bat with a gasp like he'd just come out of a trance. His chest heaved. Sweat poured down his face.

Kalli put herself between him and the car. "What are you doing? Are you trying to get arrested?"

"I—" he started, then ran both hands through his hair, his fingers shaking. "I can't—I can't take it anymore."

"Take what?" I asked, gently stepping closer. "Josh, talk to us."

He looked between the three of us, eyes wide with panic and shame. "I thought Barry was helping me. I thought this job meant I could finally stay out of trouble, but he's worse than anyone I've ever known."

I traded looks with Jaz and Kalli.

"He made me do this," Josh continued, his voice cracking. "Made me destroy the equipment last month. Said he needed to claim the insurance money. I didn't want to, but he said if I didn't, he'd tell everyone I stole it. That I was back to my old ways."

My stomach dropped.

"He made me trash his car today," he added, choking on the words. "Said it would be an easy insurance claim, and he needed the money."

"For what?" Jaz asked, her voice deadly calm.

Josh exhaled, his shoulders slumping like the weight of the world had finally crushed him. "Drugs. He's hooked. Bad. Real bad. Not just weed or pills. Fancy stuff. Designer. Stuff I've never even heard of. He said if I didn't help him, he'd make sure I'd never get into college, never get another job, never have a future."

"And you believed him?" I asked softly.

"I didn't know what else to do," he whispered. "I've been on my own since I turned eighteen. Out of the foster system and alone. I was scared, and he used that."

Kalli crossed her arms. "We're going to help you, Josh. But we need the truth. All of it."

He hesitated just a second and then said, "His supplier's a woman named Vivienne. Vivienne Noire. She's the one who gives it to him—and Lila, too. I've seen them together."

"Vivienne Noire?" I repeated. "As in mysterious fashion queen?"

Josh nodded. "She's not what she pretends to be. She always comes into town dressed up, perfect hair, sunglasses like she's hiding from the sun—and her own shame."

"Oh, my God," Jaz muttered. "Of course it's her."

I felt a bitter chill creep down my spine. Vivienne had been a mystery to us—rumors, drama, manipulation. But drugs? Dealing to Barry and Lila? Using a teenager as a pawn? And according to what Mitch found, she ran her business up and down the coast.

"We're going to take care of this," I told Josh. "But you have to promise me something."

"Anything," he said, desperate.

"No more cover-ups. You're done protecting him. You want to turn your life around? This is your line in the sand."

He nodded, his eyes glassy. "I'm done."

Kalli pulled out her phone. "Let's call Nik. And Mitch."

Jaz rubbed her forehead. "I swear, I thought after the last few days, we'd get a break from any more drama."

"We live in Clearview," Kalli said wearily. "I'm beginning to think we'll never get a break ... and I'll never get to have my wedding."

20

KALLI

I t felt strange walking into Angela's studio after everything that had happened. Just a few days ago, I was tangled up in kidnapping, blackmail, and near-death experiences. Now I was just a bride picking up her dress.

My wedding dress.

The thought gave me a flicker of warmth. The wedding was back on. Nik and I were finally finding our way through the wreckage, and today I was supposed to pick up my altered gown. A moment that should've felt joyful. A moment I'd been waiting for.

The bell above the door jingled as I stepped inside. The studio was unusually quiet, now that most of her clients had dropped her, but I planned to see my wedding through with her. She'd already made the alterations, after all. Still, I was surprised to see there was no receptionist, no steamer humming, and no soft jazz playing in the background. Just silence—and a strange tension in the air, like walking into a room that had just witnessed a fight.

"Angela?" I called out, stepping cautiously past the mannequin in the front window, draped in a half-finished tulle ballgown.

I rounded the corner toward the main fitting room and froze.

Angela was standing there, clutching a pair of oversized scissors in both hands, her eyes red and wild. My wedding dress—*my* dress—hung from the tall mirror behind her, freshly steamed, beaded, flawless. And in her trembling grasp, she raised the scissors toward it like she was about to gut a memory.

"Angela, no!" I rushed forward, my heels skidding slightly on the polished floor.

She turned sharply, her face twisted with grief and rage. "Don't come any closer, Kalli."

"Okay," I said, lifting my hands, trying to keep my voice calm. "Just ... talk to me."

"You ruined everything," she spat. "You and that drive. You gave it to the police."

I blinked. "Angela ... you knew what was on that drive. Damon had evidence against more people than just you. I couldn't keep that from the police."

Tears filled her eyes. "It wasn't supposed to be like this. Damon promised I would be fine if I helped him get new clients. He promised he would bury the evidence against me and move on."

"He lied," I said gently. "*You* lied. That's not the same as being innocent."

She let out a jagged sob. "That was in my past. I've changed!"

"That still doesn't erase what you did to gain success. We all make mistakes, and we all have to atone for them."

"He *used* me, and now you—*you*—get to walk away from this with a perfect life? A perfect dress? A perfect *wedding*?"

I took a step forward. "Angela, I don't have a perfect anything, but I do know none of this is going to fix what you're feeling."

She raised the scissors again. "Now my ex-boss suddenly reappears out of nowhere? Rejoining society like she's some kind of saint? You don't know what she was like to work for. I did all the work back then, and she took all the credit, so I took her clients. Now she's suing me for slander, Kalli. *Suing* me!"

"I heard," I said, swallowing hard. "But maybe this is your chance to come clean. To take responsibility and start over."

"I've lost everything," she whispered, her voice cracking. "My business, my reputation, every single client I've ever worked for. You have no idea what it's like to watch it all burn down around you."

"I do," I said, my voice tight with emotion. "I've had my share of failures. I've been through the ashes, Angela. But I didn't start setting fire to other people just because mine went up in smoke."

She let out a shriek, lunging toward the dress with the scissors.

I didn't think. I just moved.

We collided in a blur of satin and metal, knocking over a dress form as we tumbled to the ground. She was surprisingly strong, pure adrenaline surging through her as she fought me off. The scissors clattered to the floor and skidded under a bench.

"Get off me!" she screamed, scratching at my arms, kicking wildly. *It's not fair. None of this is fair.*

"Angela, stop before it's too late!" I grabbed her wrists, wrestling her into a sitting position, panting, my heart pounding out of my chest. "I can help you."

"I don't want your help. You're going to get what you deserve," she spat, her eyes blazing. "Just like Damon did." *I'm not sorry he's dead.*

That was all I needed to hear.

I managed to maneuver her arms behind her back and yanked a silk ribbon from a nearby hanging gown. Not ideal restraints, but strong enough for now. I tied her wrists tightly and stood, backing away as she thrashed on the floor, happy to be clear of her thoughts.

I grabbed my phone with trembling fingers and dialed.

Nik picked up on the first ring. "Kalli?"

"I'm at Angela's studio," I gasped. "She tried to destroy my dress. She—she attacked me. She said I was going to get what I deserved just like Damon did. I think she—Nik, I think she killed him."

There was a pause. "Are you okay?"

"Yeah," I said, still breathless. "I got the scissors away from her. She's tied up, but you need to come. Now."

"I'm on my way," he said, his voice cold and focused.

Ten minutes later, the front bell jingled again—and this time, it wasn't delicate or friendly. Nik stormed in with Mitch right behind him, guns holstered, eyes sweeping the studio like they expected an ambush.

I led them to the back where Angela had finally stopped struggling. She was slumped against the wall now, the fight gone from her body, her face pale and dazed.

When Nik stepped forward and read her rights, she looked up, blinking slowly. "I didn't kill him," she said, her voice suddenly small. "You have no proof."

"You said enough," I whispered. "To me."

Nik cuffed her, and Mitch led her out gently but firmly.

Nik lingered behind, checking my arms which were scratched but mostly okay. "You good?"

I nodded, tears finally welling in my eyes. "Yeah. Just ... I never thought she'd snap like that."

"Stress. Guilt. The house of cards falling in," he said. "Doesn't excuse it, but it explains it."

I looked over at my dress, still hanging in the fitting mirror, untouched. Still perfect.

But now it felt like more than just a dress. It felt like a symbol. A reminder that even after the worst storms, some things could still be salvaged.

Still be beautiful.

Sunny

If there was one thing Ophelia Ballas knew how to do better than matchmaking, it was throwing a party. She had Jasper running around putting final touches on everything as we arrived, and not so subtly pushing him in the direction of every available woman.

Poor guy.

Now that Kalli's life was settling, he didn't stand a chance.

The backyard of Kalli's parents' house looked like a page out of *Greek Life Magazine*, if such a thing existed. Blue and white streamers fluttered between the olive trees, ceramic evil eyes hung from every trellis, and tables overflowed with platters of souvlaki, spanakopita, dolmades, and of course, about six different versions of baklava. The scents of roasted lamb, lemon, and fresh oregano wrapped around us like a hug.

They always had Sunday brunch after church and

invited those of us who were like family but not Greek. This time, we had a lot to celebrate. The murderer—Angela—had finally been caught. And for the first time in what felt like forever, the laughter came easily.

Kalli sat under a canopy with Nik, Jaz, and Boomer, who was fresh out of the hospital with a sling, a few bruises, and about a thousand bad jokes he was dying to unleash. Mitch stood nearby, chatting with Father Papadopoulos and sneaking bites off my plate like he wasn't a full-grown man with his own. Jo and Zoe sat at the kids' table, trying and failing to keep Collin, Jeremiah, Tina, River, and baby Alannah from turning their plates into modern art.

Even Despina was here, sporting her big Sunday hat and loudly announcing that she made the *best* pastitsio and *no one* could change her mind. Even my parents appeared to be enjoying themselves. It felt good. *Normal.* A nice change from focusing on murder and mobsters.

Kalli stood up, clinking her glass with a spoon. "I have an announcement!"

Everyone fell silent, turning toward her with wary smiles after her *last* announcement.

She beamed at Nik, her whole face glowing. "Now that the murder is solved and life is getting back to normal—Nik and I are officially back on track. The wedding is back on!"

The whole backyard erupted into cheers and clapping. Even Father Papadopoulos offered a hearty, "To Kalliope and Nikos!" as he raised his wine glass.

Boomer whistled, causing Wolfgang to bark and Willow to start howling in excitement, setting off a chain reaction from Armani, Versaci, and Chanel over at the dog park section Kalli's pop Amos had lovingly fenced off.

Nik leaned over and kissed Kalli's hand, and even my stoic husband, Detective Grumpy Pants, cracked a smile.

I grabbed a glass of lemonade, feeling lighter than I had in weeks. Maybe this really was the beginning of a new chapter. As I moved toward one of the tables, I noticed a big bouquet of flowers—a mix of white lilies, blue hydrangeas, and bright yellow daisies—artfully arranged in a vase at the center of Ophelia's "honor table."

Wendy, dressed in a pale-yellow sundress, fussed proudly with the placement of the napkins nearby. She caught me looking and smiled. "I brought them for Ophelia," she said warmly. "As a thank you. She's always been so kind to me, including me in everything here. I wanted to give her something special for today."

"That's really sweet of you," I said. I brushed my fingers lightly against a soft blue hydrangea, admiring how fresh and vibrant the arrangement looked. And the moment I touched the petals—

It hit me like a jolt.

Blood. White fabric, stained red. Scissors—not sewing scissors, but long florist's shears—opening and closing with mechanical precision. And a cold voice whispering passionately, 'He deserved it.'

I gasped, stumbling back a step.

"Sunny?" Zoe called from a few tables away, frowning. "You okay?"

The music stopped and everyone turned to look. Even Kalli's smile faded.

I steadied myself on the table, my heart pounding. I looked at Wendy, still smiling at me, so calm. It made my blood run cold. I straightened, my voice trembling but strong enough to carry. "Angela might have snapped, even she admitted that. She might have attacked Kalli. But she's not the murderer."

A ripple of confusion moved through the yard.

Kalli stood slowly, her hand going to Nik's shoulder instinctively.

Mitch's jaw tightened.

I pointed at Wendy. "It was you," I said. "You killed Damon."

For a moment, the whole world seemed to pause. Even the cicadas stopped buzzing.

Wendy didn't even try to deny it. She just sighed, like I'd asked her to confess something mildly inconvenient. "My sister was Amy Davis," she said, her voice soft but clear. "You probably don't recognize the name. She lived in the next town over. Different last name because I was married back then."

She walked slowly around the table, running her hand across the bouquet she'd made, the scissors she'd used now hidden away.

"Damon met her when he found out his wife was cheating on him. When he was playing his games. He pretended he loved my sister, and she was gullible. Always had been. He swindled every penny she had. Promised to leave his wife for her but then left her with nothing. She had a massive heart attack from the stress. Died alone in her tiny apartment, *literally* of a broken heart, while he moved on to his next victim."

Tears filled her eyes, but her face remained calm. Detached.

"I waited a long time for this," she continued. "I waited for him to feel even a fraction of what he made her feel, but he never did. He just kept ruining lives and smiling while he did it."

Father Papadopoulos crossed himself quietly.

Jo hugged her twins tighter.

"I didn't plan to do it, not really," Wendy continued. "But when I heard what he was doing to this town, to you good people, I couldn't stand it anymore. I happened to get to the church early that fateful morning, planning to surprise Father with pruning the roses out front, when I noticed Vanessa's trunk wasn't completely closed. One can never be too safe, you know."

A small bubble of hysteria slipped out of Kalli's mouth before she pressed her lips together.

Wendy continued, "I was about to close the trunk for Vanessa, but I saw Damon alone and couldn't pass up this opportunity. It was like a divine intervention, inviting me to seek justice once and for all. I don't even remember my hand moving with my florist shears. I just remember an uncontrollable rage sweeping over me. After I realized what I had done, I closed the trunk and told myself it was justice. Mercy, even."

Zoe covered her mouth.

Kalli sat back down heavily, with Nik wrapping an arm protectively around her.

"And Angela?" I asked, my voice shaking.

"She thought everything still revolved around her drama on the drive," Wendy said. "Poor thing snapped when her life fell apart. She actually believed she could have killed him, but it wasn't her who finished Damon. It was me ... and I'm not sorry one bit."

Mitch and Nik moved toward her slowly, careful, like they were approaching a wounded animal.

Wendy didn't run. She didn't fight. She just smiled sadly and held out her wrists. "I'm ready," she said.

As Nik cuffed her and read her rights, she turned to me. "Thank you for bringing this out in the open," she said. "For giving my sister a voice, even if I have to pay the price. I have already lost everything anyway."

And just like that, the dark cloud we thought had lifted came crashing back down. But this time, we weren't broken. This time, we knew how to survive it.

Wendy stood quietly as Nik gently adjusted the cuffs. Her expression was calm—almost peaceful—but her eyes shimmered with something deeper. Regret, maybe. Or the weight of too many years pretending everything was fine.

Before she could be led away, Ophelia stepped forward, the blue hem of her polyester pants swishing around her ankles, her face drawn tight with emotion. "Wait," she said, her voice firm but trembling. "I speak now."

Nik paused, nodding.

Ophelia looked at Wendy, her eyes full of tears—not rage, not condemnation—just sorrow. "You should've told us," she said quietly. "We family. All of us. You join us for holidays, for biriba club, for Sunday service ... you one of us."

Wendy blinked, her lips parting, but she didn't speak.

"You no lose everything. You no had to be alone in you pain," Ophelia continued. "You no had to carry it like this—by youself. We would've helped you, Wendy. We *wanted* to. That what family do. Now it too late."

Chloe stepped up beside her and crossed herself, her voice soft. "Justice one thing. But secrets ... they eat you alive."

"And now look," Aunt Tasoula added with a shake of her head. "We bury another ghost in this town."

Despina sniffled, dabbing at her eyes with a lace handkerchief. "We could've cooked. We could've prayed. We could've listened. But we didn't even know."

Wendy's eyes filled with tears, and for the first time, her calm cracked. "I didn't think I deserved it," she whispered. "Not after what happened to her. Not after what I did."

Ma reached forward and gently touched her shoulder. "We all have darkness, koukla. What matter is whether you let it bury you—or whether you reach for light. We would've been you light."

A silence settled over the yard—not the kind that suffocates, but the kind that honors pain. That leaves space for grief, for forgiveness, and for the ache of what might've been.

Nik nodded softly and then guided Wendy toward the gate.

As they disappeared down the path, I felt Tina's small hand slip into mine. I looked down and saw her wide gray eyes blinking up at me.

"Was that lady bad?" she asked, clutching her junior detective badge tight.

I crouched beside her, brushing her bangs from her forehead. "She was sad, baby. And when people don't get help for their sadness, sometimes they make bad choices."

Tina nodded, thoughtful. "We help people, right?"

"We do," I said, my voice thick with emotion. "We always try."

"I'm gonna keep helping people when I grow up." She nodded once with conviction.

I smiled, believing her. "And what's River going to do?"

"Join the circus," she said without missing a beat, and then she shrugged adding, "What else would he do with magic?"

I laughed out loud at that because she was probably right.

Across the table, Kalli wiped a tear and raised her glass of lemonade. "To the people who stayed. And to the ones we couldn't save."

We all raised our glasses with her.

And Ophelia, her voice stronger now, added, "To the family we choose, not just the one we born with."

Because in Clearview, family meant more than blood. It meant showing up—especially when the pie was fresh, the grief ran deep, and the music played on.

EPILOGUE

KALLI

I t wasn't a big wedding, but it was ours.

After everything we'd survived—murder, mayhem, a briefly postponed engagement, and more dog hair than should be legally allowed—it only felt right that the wedding be small, sacred, and very, *very* Greek.

We stood outside the little Greek Orthodox church in Clearview, sunlight pouring over the white stucco and blue trim like a blessing. Bougainvillea bloomed against the stone walls, and a soft breeze fluttered the lace trim of my veil. The mamas had always imagined some huge, over-the-top affair for my wedding—ballroom, chandelier, synchronized dancing waiters—but somewhere between dodging flying scissors and surviving kidnapping, I'd learned how to say no and put my foot down for what I wanted. Something small. Something different.

Something real.

Nik stood across from me now in a perfectly tailored navy suit, his dark curls just a little windswept and his eyes so locked on mine it made my knees feel like baklava. My dress shimmered faintly in the sun, the beadwork glinting with every breath. Thank Zeus

I'd gotten it back from Angela before she could commit fashion homicide.

The mamas had cried when they saw me in it.

Father Papadopoulos stood between us, smiling with that mixture of pride and exasperation reserved for longtime parishioners and adult children who still got into trouble. Behind him, the gold icons glowed in the afternoon light.

But this moment—the one I never dared dream would happen—felt even more complete because Nik's father and extended family had flown in and Michael Flannigan stood there, too, in the second row. My biological father. The former drug addict turned Catholic priest, who'd spent the latter part of his life serving others ... and, after years apart, had found his way back to me. Some disaster during his sabbatical had kept him from contacting me for weeks, but he'd made it.

He was here.

Not to give me away—that honor belonged to the man who had raised me, my pop, and of course, Ma, who insisted on taking one arm and practically dragging me down the aisle like a prize goat at the village festival. But Michael being here, smiling quietly through misty blue eyes, meant everything to me.

And next to him stood my brother, Jasper—grinning proudly, with a camera around his neck, pretending he wasn't crying behind his aviators. We'd decided not to get a new photographer. Our families took so many pictures of every event, capturing all the memories we would ever need.

Nik and I exchanged crowns, our hands tied in white ribbon as we took our ceremonial steps around the altar—*Dance of Isaiah*, they called it. To me, it felt like finally, finally stepping into a life I had only dreamed of. I glanced down at the heirloom wedding ring on my finger and vowed to never take it off.

When Father gave his blessing, and Nik kissed me, the applause erupted from the pews—half laughter, half sniffles, all joy.

Outside, the mamas and the trio and even Vivian were already herding guests toward the tent set up on the church lawn, which looked like something out of a Mediterranean wedding magazine.

Chloe, in a seafoam-green wrap dress and a pearl necklace from her yiayia, was overseeing the welcome table with Despina, who had gone full Martha Stewart with eucalyptus garlands and gold calligraphy name cards. Aunt Tasoula had created lavender satchels for favors—homemade, of course—and the scent filled the air like a promise of peace. Ma bustled around making sure the spanakopita stayed warm and that no one moved the evil eye charms she'd zip-tied to the tent poles.

"To keep out curses," she whispered to me. "Just in case."

I smiled slightly as I studied my bouquet—let's just say *new* flowers had been arranged. Ma didn't trust hydrangeas anymore.

The reception was simple but stunning: round tables with soft linen cloths, tiny olive trees in terracotta pots for centerpieces, and strands of warm twinkle lights strung across the tent like the stars had been invited.

Jaz raised her glass first, delivering a toast that was equal parts heartfelt and hysterical.

"To Kalli and Nik," she said, her eyes misty but smiling. "May your lives be less dangerous than your engagement. May your future be full of love, laughter, and only *one* ring of wedding-related arrests."

Everyone roared with laughter, including Boomer, who stood beside her with a cane in one hand and a plate of feta in the other. "To Nik and Kalli. Don't take each other for granted. Don't go to bed angry. And if I ever need to tackle anyone else for either of you," he said, "I'd better get a second helping of lamb."

Mitch gave Nik a firm handshake-turned-bro-hug, and even Sean got misty-eyed, though he blamed it on an olive pit getting caught in his throat. Cole took it upon himself to teach the kids a dance they absolutely made up on the spot, which included dramatic slow-motion twirls and a lot of jazz hands. Tina, Jeremiah, and Collin led the charge, dragging a newly walking River giggling behind them like a flower-crowned general of chaos, with Sunny hot on his heels.

And if anyone noticed the centerpieces move on their own, they kept it to themselves.

Even baby Alannah seemed content, bouncing in Zoe's arms while Jo snuck pieces of baklava from the dessert table. Zoe caught her but just winked and said, "I won't tell if you get extra for me."

Granny Gert, Great Grandma Tootsie, and Fiona surprised everyone by serenading us in three-part harmony during the first dance with a Greek version of *Can't Help Falling in Love*. I cried into Nik's lapel, and he pulled me closer, filling my head with soothing thoughts.

And oh, the food. Long tables groaned under platters of roasted lamb, lemon potatoes, grilled vegetables, fresh bread, and tzatziki that Ma had "fixed" because the caterer didn't use enough garlic.

"Honestly," she muttered, "amateurs."

Willow, Armani, Versaci, Chanel, and Wolfgang were penned in the pet tent nearby—yes, we had a pet tent at church—with floral collars and custom bow ties. They had their own dog-safe cake, and Wolfgang snuck half of Willow's when no one was looking.

Later in the evening, Father Papadopoulos approached us at our table and placed a gentle hand on my shoulder.

"Marriage," he said, "is not the end of the journey. It is the road that begins when love is no longer a feeling, but a promise."

I nodded, squeezing Nik's hand under the table. "Then we're ready."

We sure are, Mrs. Stevens.

"Good," Father said with a smile. "But just in case, I gave your mamas more holy water." Nik chuckled. "We'll add it to our emergency kit."

As the sun dipped behind the church, painting the sky in purples and golds, we danced beneath the stars. It was a mix of traditional Greek circle dances and some modern tunes courtesy of Josh, now officially promoted to DJ and completely free of blackmail and threats since Barry had been arrested for fraud, Lila was in rehab, and Vivienne had vanished like a ghost.

Josh played with confidence, pride, and zero criminal activity.

Michael stood quietly near the tent, smiling at me across the crowd. I caught his eye, and for a second, time slipped away. It was a small thing—a nod, a smile —but it anchored me in a way nothing else ever had. I wasn't missing any pieces anymore.

My pop. My ma. My brother. My biological father. *Everyone* I loved was here.

My world was complete.

Nik pulled me close during one last dance, brushing a kiss against my forehead. "We've come a long way since we first met, Mrs. Stevens," he whispered.

"We sure have, Detective Dreamy." I looked into his eyes. "No regrets?"

"Not a single one." He slowly bent his head and kissed my lips.

I tucked my head against his chest, feeling the steady beat of his heart, the laughter and music all around us, and the blessing of being exactly where I was meant to be.

Home.

At last.

BOOKS BY KARI LEE TOWNSEND

My Big Fat Fatal Wedding

<u>DIGITAL DIVA</u>

Talk to the Hand

Rise of the Phenoteens

BOOKS BY KARI LEE HARMON

COLDWATER COVE

Dark Seas

Frozen Waters

Dangerous Thaw

Deadly Frost

STANDALONE NOVELS

Valley of Secrets

Until Tomorrow

Project Produce

Love Lessons

LAKEHOUSE TREASURES NOVELLAS

James

Amber

Meghan

Brook

MERRY SCROOG-MAS NOVELLAS

Naughty or Nice

Sleigh Bells Ring

Jingle all the Way

TRIPLE R RANCH SHORT STORIES

Destiny Wears Spurs

Spurred by Fate

PORTRAIT OF A WOMAN

Resilient

Resourceful

Rebellious

Reclusive

ABOUT THE AUTHOR

Kari Lee Townsend is a National Bestselling Author of mysteries & a tween superhero series. She also writes romance and women's fiction as Kari Lee Harmon. With a background in English education, she's now a full-time writer, wife to her own superhero, mom of 3 sons, 1 darling diva, 1 daughter-in-law & 3 lovable fur babies. These days you'll find her walking her dogs or hard at work on her next story, living a blessed life.

www.ingramcontent.com/pod-product-compliance
Lightning Source LLC
Chambersburg PA
CBHW011512100726
47899CB00010BD/3331